The Soft Landing Collection

Sapphic Fantasy and Science Fiction Stories

Jacquelynn Lyon

Dedicated to Betsy,

You told me that the moon comes out even when it's not full. I often still wax and wane, but you always taught me that I had important things to say. Thank you, I wouldn't be here without you.

Contents

The Glass Window

The first one they put in her cage was a girtablilu. He was a fiery youth with bright orange barbwire hair and a red scorpion torso ending in a nasty-looking stinger.

He looked like he would set fire to every tuft of grass and scrap of foliage in sight just to watch the visitors gape and to bask in his own flames, which he did. Paria watched him flash his hundred-watt smile her way and scorch the sand into a charred goo, almost glass and almost nothing. Paria wrinkled her nose at him and waited for the creature to tire himself out.

The satyr across the way, Foloi, snickered at her like he knew—he always knew something. She made a face at him and squared her shoulders. He just played a jaunty tune on his pan-pipes in return.

She didn't even bother to learn this girtablilu's name before summoning a familiar tingle in her fingertips, a surge of power that coursed through her. She raised the water level with a flick of her wrist and let him flounder. He tried to evaporate the waves before they hit him, but Paria jerked her chin up and sent him capsizing. He began treading water helplessly, and Paria lounged on her sandy beach a little way off.

Her caretaker, Sydney, gave her a sharp look as the other Mythic thrashed around in the deep lagoon water. The zoo surely didn't like when their fantastical merchandise, the rare Mythics, were debased. No one wanted to think of the creatures dragged from humans' deepest imaginations as fallible too.

Sydney definitely wasn't amused.

Paria just flipped her long, dark hair over her shoulder. She wasn't going to share her enclosure, and she wasn't going to be mated or bonded or subjected to whatever it was they were planning.

Foloi played some garish cartoon theme song on his pipes across from her, and a young blond girl clapped along excitedly. Paria watched for a moment, the young girl's pink, tiny hands clumsily coming together again and again. Foloi smirked when he noticed her. Paria groaned at herself and rubbed her temples before diving to the bottom of her cage.

They fished out the girtablilu with a crane later that day, the young thing looking like a drowned shadow of himself afterward. He shot her a dejected look on the way out.

I'm not sorry, she said to herself. *I'm not going to balance a ball on my nose and clap my flippers together when they ask.* Especially when it came to being pair bonded, she wasn't a deer befriending a tiger for visitors' amusement.

They left her alone for another week.

$$\infty\infty\infty$$

Paria's enclosure was taller than it was wide, consisting of a sandy bank that fed into a little grassy area with several small bushes and a single "lovely" peach tree. Her mom loved peaches, though she never made it to this enclosure.

The beach dropped off quickly into deep, salty water that was made to resemble the sparkling robin's-egg blue of her "natural" habitat. It was warm, and the back side of her cage was made to look like bumpy rocks. It faced a long length of glass that separated her from an indoor visitor hallway. Her other wall was simply dark and empty, a large expanse of wall with a length of glass at the bottom that separated her from the next cage.

The topside was surrounded by a red railing that visitors could lean on, cameras out, mouths hanging open, squeals of joy and surprise erupting as she breached. Phone cameras clicked, capturing the ideal mermaid: long, wavy brown hair with small braids threaded with gold. Long, slim wrists, prettily browned skin, and a round face and full lips—a Pacific Islander.

She was the pride of the zoo, or perhaps that's just what they told her. She did enough sneering at the cameras to break them, after all.

Paria didn't know why they kept bothering to put new Mythics in her cage. She managed to take out the naga and kinarra with a swish of her tale and a little creativity with water on the kinarra's feathers. The naga almost strangled her, but they struck a deal in the end: He wasn't interested in being paired for show either. They turned the tank upside down, tearing up grass, displacing sand, making a general mess. Sydney eventually intervened and signed with her hands to Paria that she might as well knock it off.

Paria had a feeling it was the zoo's idea to make an exhibit of two different Mythics pairing off, but she wasn't going to have Sydney or management walking all over her. It wasn't their business if she stared out her tank window and blew depression bubbles to the top of the water.

I don't need any strange zoo transfer boys pushed on me, thinking they can woo me with a poem and a compliment to insert-body-part-of-the-day. I know I'm pretty; I don't need a second opinion. She scowled at nothing. *And I don't need any interventions.*

So Paria lingered at the bottom of her tank, blowing fine, crystalline bubbles to the surface one by one and getting lost in her own thoughts. The bubbles were a sign of discontent, though she knew the zoo couldn't figure out why. *Let them never know.*

The "issue" arose around two months earlier.

Paria saw her the first time when the moon was a slim crescent smile up above and the adjacent hallway was nothing but an echoing ghost walk. She liked being awake during those times. The guest halls bore long shadows and a deep silence. She could be alone with her thoughts and so many other things.

Or, at least, she thought she was alone.

Paria always assumed there was something huge and sinister in the tank next to hers. The water there was dark and vast —an impenetrable black contrasting her perfect, soft blue—and the glass was cold and silent beside her. It was lower than hers, only a large plexiglass window separating the bottom of her tank with the top of theirs.

Perhaps a miniature kraken or electric squid lived there, but she didn't know. Paria always figured the deep-sea creatures would shine their fanged teeth at her at some point and she would have nightmares. She avoided that faceless, seven feet of glass on most nights, but maybe tonight she felt like having nightmares.

Paria swam back and forth along the bottom, running her hands over oysters and counting in her head how long another pearl would take to form in them. That was one of her enrichment programs: diving for pearls and collecting shells. She figured the zoo thought those were appropriate activities for her. Now all she needed to do was play the harp and listen to their money buckets fill. She wasn't going to play the harp.

The pearls themselves could be lovely, though. She wasn't completely opposed to the smooth, misshapen lumps in her hands and their off-colored ivory sheen. It made her want to start a hoard and pretend to be a dragon instead of a nascent mermaid. She could be a pearl dragon, ten feet—no, twenty feet —tall and sitting on her growing hoard until she kissed the sky and disappeared completely. It was a pleasant dream to pass the time.

Paria ran her hands along the spine of one of her oysters and her eyes unfocussed. This one would be ready soon. Perhaps she would weave it into the seams of her belt with the others.

Her vision was blurry and distant when she caught a flash of light in the corner of her eye, a bright burst that struck her across the face. She turned her head slowly, her skin prickling as she rotated in place. An electric surge flared in the cage next to her. She frowned.

She didn't know much about the adjacent enclosure. On some level, she never really wanted to know. She waited for a moment, pausing as she gazed into the inky waters of the deep-sea cage, dark and unknowable.

The water was still and calm, fathomless. Shivers ran from her tail to her fingertips as the same distant light sparked through the dark like a beacon. Paria raised her eyebrows. *I doubt that light can be anything good,* she said to herself.

Nonetheless, despite herself, Paria pushed off the cage floor and tentatively approached the edge. She furrowed her brow. *I've lived in the shadow of this place too long.* She was drawn to the side. She waited for another minute, body still and treading water.

Did I imagine it? she wondered, considering if she had really just seen a strip of lightning beside her. She hummed for a moment. *Maybe I should just go back up.*

Then a white light like a flash bomb illuminated a long, twisting figure. Paria hovered closer and craned her neck. *Something is in there, and close,* she thought with a slight tremble.

The murky outline of something curved took shape in front of her. She pressed herself up against the glass and tried to make out as much of it as she could.

It was long, with a mop of something swirling around its head, like kelp or a storm cloud. She couldn't make out the full form. She squinted. It wasn't huge like she had expected.

Paria waited, pursing her lips and flicking her tail anxiously back and forth. Finally, the next brilliant flash erupted, a blip of light seeping into the depths, a fading white sunset. It illuminated a single silhouette.

Paria's breath hitched. She could see it was humanoid. Humanoid with a long scaled tailed and a pair of gills on its neck. Paria's pulse sped up. It was like her, *like her.* The striking profile made her dizzy.

The other creature had wild, flowing red hair that swirled

around her, almost as if it, too, were alive. Her skin was a similar brilliant red against flushed black stripes on her sides and arms. Her tail was a flashing dark maroon, and she had eyes like wide pools of milk. Paria's mouth was hanging open, her mind racing. It was another mermaid.

They didn't bother to cover her up with a shell bra like they did Paria. She hovered, naked and raw in the water, a lithe length of coiled muscles and bright white, fanged teeth. She was made of hard edges and jagged points, instead of the soft brushstrokes expected of Paria.

The mermaid had a series of spikes along her spine and a tail that whipped around the water like a razor. Her face was something sharp and almost alien. She had the same mouth as Paria and a lovely, round cherry nose under a pair of wide starry eyes.

It was ghoulish and breathtaking in one gasping vision. Paria's thoughts sparked and ran into each other. She couldn't help but feel her heart squeeze, almost painfully.

What is that?

∞∞∞

She had a sense of it deep in her bones, but she couldn't put a name to it. There was another mermaid—another mermaid filled with pointed teeth and something electric.

She tried to dismiss it for the night. The figure disappeared in one bat of her powerful tail a second later as Paria pushed off the sandy bottom and rose quickly to the surface. She gulped down the sharp, cold air of the night and let it shock her into clarity. She panted breathlessly, staring at the moon until her senses came back to her.

It's just another mermaid, she reminded herself, eyes wide and breath coming out in short rapid bursts. *We're separated even.*

She went to sleep that night with a ringing in her ears and

some deep itch in her veins. She could feel a restlessness take root in her core. Something was different now.

The image started to haunt her waking thoughts. Every time she closed her eyes, it played like a movie in the back of her head. A red mermaid with black, glowing stripes. Paria would like to glow. Paria would like to *something.*

They were not necessarily nightmares, but something else entirely.

She started floating loosely by the glass window at the bottom of the enclosure, watching the nothingness of the next cage over.

It was still mostly dim and empty, but sometimes faint lights were visible during the day. Bright LEDs turned on so the guests could catch a glimpse of the deep and get some sort of brief thrill. Maybe that's what Paria was looking for too.

She waited at the side of her cage by her oysters and swore she kept seeing the frame of wild, red hair and a lightning spine. She saw that and nothing else; she saw nothing.

Paria started to eat less and blow bubbles from the bottom of her cage.

∞∞∞

By the tenth day after the sighting, Paria decided to suck up her pride and float up to her caretakers, post-feeding. They had their heads close together and were gesturing toward the water. She had a feeling they were discussing her, but she tried to ignore it. She mostly wanted to ignore them for the rest of her long life, but she stifled that impulse for just one moment.

She was known for being moody anyway.

She popped up quickly and started signing furiously before she even knew if they were watching. Sydney focused on her with an even look.

Paria moved her hands. "Who is that?" she said, pointing loosely toward the far wall.

Sydney raised an eyebrow. Paria rarely signed to them. It was her mother who had been the talkative one. She had learned from her but had not taken up the chatterbox mantle.

Sydney knelt and signed slowly back to her, as if they were rusty, "Who?"

Paria sunk a little lower in the water and narrowed her eyes. She smothered her ego and pointed more clearly toward the right, to the next tank over.

Maya raised her eyebrows behind Sydney and whispered something to other the woman, who seemed to brush it off.

Sydney smiled back gently, her face relaxing into something like understanding.

What are they possibly happy about? Paria wondered, her whole body tensing.

Sydney moved closer to the shoreline and started signing to Paria, "That is Riga. She lives with the other deep-sea Mythics."

Paria sank down in the water again with only her eyes showing, watching Sydney carefully and waiting for more information. Sydney just smiled down at her. Paria thrashed her tail.

Unsatisfied, Paria rose again to use her hands. "Who is she?" she asked.

Sydney signed back right away. "A mermaid," she expressed quickly, "like you."

Paria bit the inside of her cheek and was torn between asking more questions and going to hide underneath a rock. Before she could decide, she saw the zoo's aquarium manager approach.

"Is Paria being friendly today?" he asked. "She is such a beaut in this light."

Paria snarled briefly and swam down before she had to endure any more words from them. She didn't need it. She blinked at the bottom window, examining the long slices of dark glass.

Riga the mermaid, deep-sea Riga.

∞∞∞

Paria was situated with her belly on the sand floor and her chin propped up. Her vision glazed over as she kept her usual watch on the bottom window, ignoring the steady tapping of a toddler on the glass next to her. Her perch was more routine now than anything. She occasionally blew another bubble to form a thick sea foam above her.

She was in the middle of a long daydream about fashioning a rope out of the flowers the enrichment program gave her when she saw it: a river of violent red hair. A bloody twisting sunrise around that ghoulish, barely-there face. Riga rose from the depths like a mirage.

Paria could feel her mouth making a small O shape. *She is lovely,* she thought. Lovely in the dark, glowing gently against the bright sheen of Paria's lagoon water as she stared flatly ahead, directly at her and unmoving. Statuesque.

Paria opened her mouth uselessly. All she could look at was Riga's long, jagged stripes across her body and her lithe, muscled limbs and a wiry torso ending in a powerful tail. Riga probably wasn't made to dive for pearls.

Paria tried to sign something, to do anything, but her muscles tensed. All she could do was feel her temperature rise slowly, slowly . . . and then she felt like she was burning up from the inside out. Riga still looked at her with an expressionless gaze, and Paria quickly turned around.

She wasn't ready. She suddenly felt like she was having her day-nightmares all over again, and, panicking, she swam to the top of her enclosure in five strokes with her face on fire.

This didn't feel normal; this didn't feel like just an empty pastime right then.

She beached herself on the sandbank and planted her head facedown in the dirt. Visitors inquired if she was sick.

∞∞∞

Paria had her regularly scheduled doctor's appointment the next week. She was almost relieved. Maybe they would cure her of her sudden aching thoughts.

She hadn't seen Riga since then, or at least, not in person —she relived over and over that second of closeness and the hot tingle throughout her fingers and skin.

Paria was willing to give her doctor another chance.

She let him examine her pulse and lungs, prod at her sea bladder and scales. They weighed her with a great effort to get her on the scale. (They liked to keep her weight low, apparently.) She was *easy* for once, and even Dr. Schlotman's interest seemed piqued.

He took her temperature last and hummed thoughtfully as she sat on his sturdy metal table.

Maya cleared her throat and Paria glanced between all three humans in the room. "I know, right?" Maya said with her palms up. "This is barely Paria."

The doctor seemed to hum again.

"We just have to know if anything's wrong," Sydney chimed in, and Paria suddenly experienced a brief wave of gratitude toward her.

Dr. Schlotman slowly, carefully, took out the thermometer from her underarm and looked at it thoughtfully. "It's not that unusual," he said, shaking it, "though, truthfully, I never thought this one would ever show."

Maya gave him a concerned look. "Show, like what?"

The doctor chuckled. "I thought you would know."

Sydney cleared her throat. "We would be very interested in knowing now then."

He nodded curtly. "She is showing all the signs of something akin to . . . well"—he chuckled awkwardly again—"pair-bonding cycles."

Paria's cheeks flared, and she wished none of them were paying any attention to her.

Sydney's eyes widened. "That's impossible," she said finally. "She's never been exposed to any pheromones. She's never even had a fecundity ceremony with a school."

The doctor tilted his head to the side. "She's more than matured, isn't she?"

Maya sniffed and eyed her. "More than mature, yeah, but ..."

"These things happen," the doctor said as he stood up and looked between all three of them. "Of course, she's not showing all of the symptoms, but her temperature and hormones are evidence enough."

Sydney seemed to swallow thickly. "We can't introduce any mermen to her tank. They'll attack her." Sydney and Maya both glanced at her shredded right fin, a ragged imitation of the real thing. "She gets around fine with her hydrokinesis, but others will have that too. They'll try and take her out."

From what Paria understood, unrelated mermaids did not tolerate weakness or defects in others; it would slow down their school. Her stomach sank. *Maybe even deep-sea ones with blazing red hair would feel that way,* she pondered.

She looked at her hands bitterly for a long moment.

"Who said anything about more mermen?" the doctor said in an even tone.

Paria looked up pointedly, and a quiet kind of static overtook the room.

"I suppose we could try other types of Mythics," Maya finally spoke up slowly, "just to emotionally pair with. Nothing more."

The three shared a glance while Paria glared at them and signed something angrily. They ignored it.

They introduced the first suitor to her cage the following week. It didn't end well.

∞∞∞

Paria spent a couple more weeks brooding, kicking suitors out, and lounging by cool spots in her cage to keep her temperature down. It took her another day to hesitantly approach the glass window again. She practiced in her head what she wanted to say, what she wanted to try to communicate, what to try at all.

For some reason, Paria had a notion Riga had answers of some sort.

And it's not like she can attack me through the glass, she thought as she swam to the bottom of her cage. And she waited, almost gnawing through her bottom lip, hoping this might be the night. She waited for two more.

When Riga finally emerged from the dark depths of her cage, she was turned away from Paria, her long body and lit-up spine a shock of brightness in the dark of night. Paria flared her gills and tried to steady her heartbeat.

Riga didn't pause in her distant motion, but Paria gradually, slowly, went to press her hand against the cool glass, keeping her eyes on Riga. Steadying her shaking fingers, she managed a single firm tap, loud and distinct.

The oscillation of the glowing white bioluminescence didn't cease, and Paria began to tap again. Her mother taught her this, human sign language first, and then the universal Pacific language second. It was technically meant to be clicked, a snap of her tongue and sound from deep within her chest—humans described it as something like a dolphin noise. But it could be translated easily enough into taps and steady beats from her fingertips, like Morse code.

She let out a rusty series of taps, etching a sloppy "hello" in three syllables.

The light stopped, it's flickering increased, and then it stopped again and turned around.

"Hello," Paria tapped again. She felt her heartbeat pound

in her wrist. She didn't know what she was doing.

The next moment felt like an eternity. Then she froze when the light flashed in her direction, starting to draw closer toward her. The flaring red hair materialized from the emptiness.

Riga approached with ease, her movements sure and unhurried as she made her way to her side of the glass. Paria earnestly searched her face for something. She went to tap on the glass again, but Riga had already put her hand there.

"Hello," she tapped back.

Paria could have practically done a summersault. There Riga was, and she wasn't even glaring at her. She just looked pleasantly ahead, curiously. Paria knew the other mermaid could understand her.

"Who is this?" Riga finally tapped with deft, easy fingers. Paria put her mind to work, sorting out her unclear knowledge of Pacific language.

She hesitantly made a couple more clumsy sounds: "Like you."

Riga tilted her head to the side, and her huge, milky eyes flicked down. Paria jerked her powerful tail back and forth to show her.

"You have a tail," Riga tapped, looking surprised. "Are you from . . . the Trench?"

Paria shook her head, but she wasn't sure that reached her. "I'm from here," she finally tapped out with a frown. "My mother was from a reef, though."

Paria watched Riga make a sharp, pointed smile, and her heart fluttered.

Riga touched the glass and looked strangely entertained. "A lagoon swimmer, of course."

Paria squirmed back and forth. "And who are you?" she asked.

Riga's smile faltered. "The Trench." She tapped back briskly, "I thought I was all alone here."

Paria slowly, tentatively put her whole hand on the thick

plexiglass; it almost matched up with Riga's. "You aren't," she said.

Riga gave another bright and surreal smile as she tapped slowly. They began to talk.

Riga explained she was from the ocean, the real ocean, but she had pierced one of her lungs in a fight with a beaked squid and woke up at the zoo with a team of specialists hovering over her.

"I wish they hadn't rescued me," she said.

"I understand," was all Paria could respond with. Next, Paria tried to introduce herself.

She was named after a body of water, as all the aquatic Mythics were in the zoo. She and her mother were taken in almost immediately after Paria was born, after she was injured. Her mother adored the caretakers, the pearls, the faces of the passing strangers. Paria could only guess at why—maybe it was the safety; maybe it was the fact Paria was healthy and alive here.

Riga smiled fondly at that as she tapped, "You must miss her."

Paria's mouth tightened and she looked down at the sandy bottom. "Do you miss anyone?" she asked as she stroked the window.

Riga paused and pursed her thin lips. "They're gone." She continued slowly, painfully, "They cast me out before I was attacked."

Paria flinched at that and nodded. She only began again after a long pause. "What's the ocean like?" she asked, changing the subject.

The faint smile returned to Riga's face. "Big."

Paria laughed at that and she saw Riga's chest shake too.

"Wonderful. Cold, warm. It smells like every corner of the world." Riga seemed to make something like a sigh. "I miss the currents most . . . and the surface. I miss the surface too."

She seemed sad, and Paria lifted her chin. "They don't let you go up?"

She shrugged and then looked away. "Let me tell you more about the ocean."

She began to spin tales of large anglerfish and epic waters and diving deeper than her wildest dreams. The ocean was vast and chilled and dangerous, she said. Paria could only watch her carefully and sigh.

Riga's smile tugged at the edges of her mouth.

"Maybe you can go back," Paria finally tapped back at her.

"Perhaps," she said, tilting her head, "though I'm not sure I'd like to be alone out there."

Paria lifted her chin to study her face. "Well," she tapped one by one, "at least we aren't alone in here."

Riga pressed herself up against the glass. "You are too sweet, young one—"

"Hey!" Paria narrowed her eyes at her. "Not that young."

"You have spirit!" Riga looked both ways and then pointed at a glowing red exit sign in the indoor hall. "The morning lookers will be here soon."

Paria nodded. Maybe she didn't need the strangers gawking at their communication. Who knew what they might think it meant.

"Maybe I'll ask my trainers to give you extra tuna," Paria joked with a slight clip to her taps, "as thanks for listening to me."

Riga pressed her fingers lightly to the glass. "No," she said easily. "No thanks needed." She smiled. "I'm the one who's glad to meet you."

That's when Paria's face flared up again. They both said goodbye, and Paria had to go bury her head in the sand a second time. When she emerged again, she couldn't stop smiling.

Paria wanted to talk to Riga every moment of every day; she wanted to ball up her fists and break down the barrier in a hundred little glass shards; she *wanted.* She didn't, however. She restrained herself and relegated herself to their nighttime visits and then sleeping during the day.

The aquarium managers were not happy about that. Mermaids were supposed to be awake.

Paria was too floored to care. She started to tell Riga everything—about her trainers, about her mom, about the satyr across the way who annoyed her but was still basically her closest friend here.

Riga slowly told her about her fight with a beaked squid who punctured her lung; she told her about sharks and starfish and riding the currents all across the world. Paria could only watch her face twitch, her body tread water easily across from her. Riga.

Paria's trainers liked that she was smiling more. They didn't like that her temperature was rising. Paria didn't know what to tell them, so she didn't tell them anything. *My body heat is none of their business,* she told herself as they looked at the thermometer and then looked at her.

It was only when Riga mentioned something offhand that Paria paused to consider her caretakers again. Riga mentioned the sun.

She tapped her response to Riga: "What's that about the sunset?"

Riga tilted her head to the side and then tapped back on the window, "During the dark months, I would go to the straits, and the sun would go down across the ice. It was"—she paused —"lovely."

"Straits?" Paria started, thinking.

"It's like the ocean, but smaller. More land around us."

"I thought you were deep sea?" Paria asked curiously. As she took in Riga's fearsome features and vivid stripes, the idea of seeing her anywhere else felt strange.

Riga's lips twitched up. "Of course, we breech." She shook her head. "I'm still a mermaid. I have lungs for a reason."

"Oh." Paria felt a little silly now as she thought about it.

"They don't let you go up?"

Riga looked the other way, scratching her chin thoughtfully. "Only for the checkups. So not really."

Paria began to clear her mind. "Idiots," she tapped a couple times.

Riga laughed again. "It's all right," she said. "From what you've told me, at least I get to hide in here. All the watching you have to go through!"

Paria clenched her jaw. "They're idiots too."

Riga nodded with a small twitch. "I'm sure it's just 'cause you're very pretty."

Paria's whole body felt like it was on fire. She tapped "idiot" again, and her insides were in a frenzy by the time the lookers arrived. There was only so much she could handle.

∞∞∞

Paria beached herself next to her handlers the following day, preparing herself mentally for the scenario she wanted: a quick talk, some bargaining.

She made a pointed look at Maya first. She was the softest and gave Paria extra trout on odd days.

"Something up, Paria?" she asked slowly, both signing and talking at once.

Paria signed feverishly. "Riga," she said several times in a row. "Riga."

"Oh." Maya blinked. "I forgot we told you about her. What about Riga?"

"She needs to come up," Paria signed with a slow clarity.

"Come up where?" Maya tilted her head to the side.

"What's all this?" Sydney asked next as she brought Paria's bucket of chum for the day.

Maya glanced at her. "Paria is talking about Riga."

"What?"

Maya turned back to her. "Where does Riga need to go?"

Paria searched the air. "Up." She pointed. "She needs to breech."

"Huh," Maya said as she put her hands on her hips. "I've never seen her concerned like this."

"She wants the deep-sea mermaid to come to the surface?" Sydney gave her a look.

"She's still a mermaid," Paria signed with a fierce flick of her wrists that made Sydney chuckle a little. "Lungs."

Sydney furrowed her brow. "That's a good point," she said.

"What's got into you, Par?" Maya asked. Then she whispered to Sydney before signing to Paria, "Where's this coming from?"

Paria began to push herself back into the water and glared at them. "Just do it, or it'll be ... bad." Paria started to submerge her head.

"Hmm." Maya turned to Sydney before Paria fully went under. "I guess we'll be talking to the deep-sea handlers."

∞∞∞

Paria had to wait another week before anything happened. She kept talking to Riga, but she didn't mention what she did.

Riga told her about some changes on the sixth day. "My handlers are acting funny," she said.

Paria grinned. "How funny? They good at it?"

Riga rolled her large, starry eyes. "Ha ha," she tapped. "No, they've been doing my vitals twice this week, and they were talking about some 'cage,' a new one. Maybe." Riga concentrated. "I'm not that great at translating still." Her handlers had been teaching Riga basic English since she got here, but Paria knew it was a steep learning curve.

Paria looked to the side. "I could talk to them. I know human language well."

Riga shook her head. "Not for me. I'm sure it's nothing

big." She leered a little with her pointy grin. "Maybe they just think I'm getting old."

Paria wrinkled her nose. "Nonsense!" she tapped with gusto. "I bet you could take down a whale."

Riga laughed. "Just for you then. A whole whale."

It was a very good night.

The next morning, Paria saw a cage placed just outside of her exit tunnel, roomy and glass. Paria scowled at it and signed to Sydney that she didn't need another checkup.

Sydney rolled her eyes and told her, "Get in the tube, silly girl. It's a surprise."

"Ugh!" Paria made a sharp noise at her, and everyone else plugged their ears at the squawk. Sydney just gave her a relaxed, shooing motion. Paria sniffed and swam the slowest she could into the next cage.

Sydney shook her head. "Don't think I haven't been watching the night tapes, girly." She winked.

Paria's mouth fell open. Her hands moved clumsily. "What?"

Sydney just turned around.

The transport was slow and rocky, taking its time sloshing her back and forth in the waters, moving her across the hallways, with the early-morning light to her back. They made their way outside and into the cool, misty daylight. She saw a high wooden fence. It said "exhibit in progress."

Paria scowled—this was the old wishing-well exhibit. She made a face at her handlers as they walked beside the dolly. She crossed her arms across her chest stubbornly.

The wishing-well exhibit used to house the talking trout, Jeremy, who passed away three months ago. The cage was deep and filled with rocks; she knew that much. She pushed her hair back. They were probably just going to keep her there while they added another frilly chair to her enclosure or a harp for her to play.

She lashed her tail angrily as they opened up the side of the transport cage and she eased reluctantly into it. "Ugh!" She let them know she was less than happy.

Sydney nudged her forward and signed, "Go."

Paria did a small circle in her new rocky enclosure before she saw another round pool next to hers. Her eyebrows rose. It was a second pool, separated by a stone arch and connected by an underwater tunnel down below. She looked at it curiously.

Her handlers turned to leave, and Paria tried to peer into the depths. A slash of white came from down below. Paria practically gasped.

She scrambled away as a fiery redhead surged up and flipped her hair back in one swooping movement. Paria almost buckled into the water.

Riga did a little spin in place and stretched her arms wide up to the sky. She smiled as broadly and brilliantly as the universe itself, and Paria could only gape. Riga turned slowly, making a happy trilling sound and swimming up to lean on the stone archway. Paria gulped, marveling at the closeness.

"You did this," Riga clicked fervently with her tongue. "I know you did."

Paria's face was on fire, and she could only shrug and click hesitantly back. She wasn't used to making the sound. "It was the right thing to do." She wiggled back and forth in the water. "You wanted it."

She jumped as she felt a touch, a calloused hand grab her own. Riga's face was wild with something. "Paria," she clicked and leaned forward, "nice to meet you."

"Nice," she went slowly, "nice not to be behind glass." She inched a little closer. "I never dreamed we could ..."

"Yes."

Paria's fever almost broke into a volcano when she felt a pair of lips peck her on the cheek. *Oh.* Her jaw went slack. Riga kissed her cheek again, a little more to the center now.

A dopey grin sprung across her face. She flipped her hand over to hold Riga's properly, feeling her rugged, bright skin, and they drew closer and closer.

She leaned in. The glass was gone.

Little Lights

I was seven years old, seven and three days, staring out over sloping, uneven hills cradling crowds of people under an inky black night. Colorful tents, squat booths, and fairy lights were set up at the very bottom of the hills while a stream of commotion was just beginning to gurgle. The air was thick with the smell of frying vats of butter, roasted meats, and the lazy heat of summer radiating off the throngs of people. It was the type of evening that gave grandmas a headache and children buzzing, sleepless nights.

I was dressed in my Sunday best, a green dress with a fat yellow bow tied around the back, buckled black shoes, and neat white socks that kept slipping down my heels. It was the type of outfit that reminded me of the smell of crusty potpourri and old lady's hand cream. My hair was tied in complex knots, braided and slicked and held back by green ribbons. I pulled on the knots with a certain vigor, trying to dislodge the tight coils and chew on the ends. It was a bad habit my mom had been trying to cut out for years with no success, even after threatening to break out a spritz bottle like you do with pets that scratch the furniture.

I had worn the same outfit three days ago at my birthday and the newness of the festival and lingering birthday rush surged sugar sweet in my veins. I craned my neck back and stared at the winking sky, expectant. Minutes passed as I tugged on my hair with one hand and held onto my mother's skirts with the other. My mother had on a colorful orange skirt and a fitted white blouse; she was tall and slender like a solid willow tree. She stood with her broad shoulders hunched and hands busy on a black camera with too many clicking buttons and a lens long enough to take an eye out. My father walked around in aimless circles behind us, muttering to himself. He was a be-spectacled man with a busy look to him—busy and graying ra-ther purposefully around the temples. He was still looking for the "perfect" patch of grass to finally set our blanket down on.

Neither of them looked up when it first appeared: a dark, lumpy mass on the horizon, rumbling toward us like an incom-ing storm cloud, heavy and huge beyond imagination. I held my breath like it might fall out of the sky if I exhaled even a little. I knew about floating continents by then, about how they stayed up, but with the lights and the crowds and the moonless pool of sky above, anything was possible.

I sucked on my bottom lip instead of my hair and tried to keep my eyes fixated on the glowing, jagged shapes of the dis-tant island. I imagined a thousand birds lifting it up into the sky and a thousand hands pushing it up from below, hoisting an en-tire mountain into the clouds.

My sister called me *over-imaginative* at that age, but that was one of the nicest things she called me overall. She was with her first boyfriend that year, somewhere up terribly high—high enough she claimed to touch the bottom of the land mass. I doubted it. I didn't believe anything could reach that high.

My mouth fell open as the sleek machine gently glided closer and closer. The continent was poised against faint stars, outlined in a fantastical, twisting design, trees and buildings and little suggestions of people coming into view. And the lights.

They slowly appeared: honey yellow, glacial blue, cherry red, burnt orange, all the crayon colors I could think of and more. They lit up one by one as hovering flames against the dark. It was a dream of a dream, and my eyes itched as I refused to blink.

My mother told me this happened every twelve months

or so, but I wasn't listening as the lanterns were gently, slowly, carefully released from the darkness. Passed into the breeze from unknown hands to an unknowing world, the way animal caretakers released rescued birds into the wild. Clueless if they'll survive or not but doing it all the same.

My eyes traced the numerous glowing patterns: polka dot ones, floral stripes, splattered paint, and some completely covered in flaking silver glitter. The second they took sail, thunderous cheering erupted around me. The crowds clapped like they wanted to make their hands sting and voices ache as they welcomed the release with fever-thick whooping.

I didn't move. My eyes were drawn to a light-pink one, pansy pink, kissed-sunset pink, pink like my little fairy princess set.

"Mommy!" I called shrilly. "That one's mine."

My mother frowned slightly. "Winnie—" she warned.

I let go of her skirts. "I have to go get it!"

"Winnie!" She grabbed for the back of my green dress. "You'll miss the paper airplanes. Don't you want to see—"

"It's my birthday lantern. Look at it." I understood birthdays in that way and nothing less. I needed it, and I was told I was too young to send up a paper airplane anyway. I blocked out the rest of what my mom said, which was probably a deep groan and potential bribery, and escaped into the sweeping crowd. I was always too fast for her, my spindly legs and buzzy movements a hinderance to old mothers and distracted fathers.

Skirts and dresses and baggy pants floated around my head, people shifting out of my way as I burst through their ranks like an exploded party popper. I had to keep my eyes on the light-pink lantern. I chased the thing as it twisted gracefully in the breeze with all the others.

"Winnie!" My mom attempted a short pursuit.

I rushed to the side, ducking my head under a low fence and skidding my knees as I scrambled away from the glow of the festival and my mom's voice. I called softly up as I ran, "Come here, little light!"

I dirtied my hands on a slope as I scurried up its side and joined a smattering of wayward youths set up on one of the steeper hills. They laughed and jumped as the first lanterns floated into reach, their brilliant smiles illuminated by a whole spectrum of descending colors. My pink one hung just above the rest, gliding sweetly down, and taking its time to end its brief, crowning journey.

"Come here!" I flailed my arms above my head and ran around in oblong circles, trying to guess where it was going to finally drop. A sudden wind picked up, carrying it above my fingertips, and I whined in the back of my throat. It was almost gone again.

"Please," I called to it firmly, "don't be difficult now." That was a phrase my grandma used when I refused to put on my jacket or touch her weird ointments. I reached up on my tip-toes. The pink lantern dropped loosely like it had been tapped from above, and my fingers curled around the panel on the very bottom.

My heart soared as I clasped it tightly, barely touching its smooth corners before gravity took hold. I tumbled backward, still clinging to the lantern as I fell onto my backside and landed with a soft *oof*. The grass no doubt stained the back of my neat skirts, and I didn't care. My eyes were glued to my glowing prize.

"Yes!" I cheered and sat gingerly up, a smile spreading like a heat wave across my face. The lantern was pink poppies, sweet jam, little dog's noses. And there was a folded note inside.

"RELEASE!" A cannon shot boomed, accompanied by silver chimes, and I looked up just in time to see the end of the ceremony. The city metro launched thousands of colorful paper airplanes back at the floating cloud city, a cascade of returning gifts. Distant cheering answered from the people on the island, probably trying to catch the planes themselves.

I couldn't stop smiling. I turned my attention back to my new lantern. "Hello, little light." I reached inside, avoiding the tinted LED bulb and curiously taking out the piece of paper.

The paper wasn't the point of the excitement for me, but

I squinted at it anyway. I knew some people sent things down with their light. I skimmed the text.

Dear anyone,

It was written with large, curling letters, each letter an alternating color, like a rainbow racing across the page. Everything seemed carefully chosen and formed. I was impressed.

I hope you get this!!! My name is Daisy. This is my lanturn. :)
It's the same color as my fairy castle and I piked it out myself.
I live in Titros and have 2 parents and 1 cat. He is a fat cat named Marshmellow. I love him and he's very old. I wished he would have kittens, but mommy says he can't. I feel very sorry for him when he mews to go outside and we don't let him outside.
I would want to go outside if I was a cat—even if I couldn't swim or play with dogs.
I go to scool every day and want to be an artist or detektiv one day. I have a detektiv glass and hat and 2 crimes already!
One is who stole Stacy's bike (not me) and the second is who nocked over the grass hut I built at the park.
Here is some of the grass I found at the crime scene!
Please enjoy my lanturn. My mom says this is a very specile time of year, and I really really want someone to find it and keep it like in the movies.
PS—Do you have a cat? Has it had kittens?
PSS—Do you think breakfast cereal is okay to eat out of a big cup? I think it's weird, but okay if it's a really big cup.
PSSS—Please be careful with my lite! I spend a lot of time on it, and I hope you love it too. :D

I held the note to my chest and lay back down in the tufts of grass. Lanterns and paper airplanes that didn't make it to their destinations fell to earth behind me. The music swelled at the bottom of the hills and the night burst with a steady, thumping beat and hammering base below. The party had just begun.

The floating continent passed slowly overhead. Its dark underside reflected the land in its shiny, black hover panels and resembled a honeycomb flattened out and dyed in plastic ink. I barely took another breath. My parents would be looking for me, but I was wondering how I was going to tell Daisy that I got her lantern and was going to take good care of it.

I was grounded for two weeks after I ran away during the festival and stained my nice clothes. I didn't mind being grounded because it just meant I couldn't play outside and couldn't use the internet.

I could still use my toys and the paint program on my computer, plus my mom didn't take down my fort, so I was okay. She didn't know why I liked my fortress so much anyway and why I wouldn't stop crying the first time they took it down. They let me keep it in the corner of my room after that, as long as I didn't try to bring it to the living room again.

I built my fortress with two sheets and a large blanket I snuck out of the linen closet. Four pillows propped up the corners and the desk and lamp held up everything else. I added a nest in the middle of it made up of stuffed toys and two enormous pillows I squished under my chest and flopped on top of.

It was three days after the festival when I crawled into the soft insides of my fort, like entering the belly of a big animal, and started writing back to Daisy.

Dear Daisy,

I sat for a very long time excitedly going over what I wanted to tell her. I had my sister check over all the spelling before I tried to write a final version of a return letter.

I found your lamp!! It is the best color. I love pink. It's my favorite color. How old are you? You sound like you're about my age.

That's good. I don't have a lot of kids my own age.

That wasn't exactly true, but it was true enough. I didn't consider myself part of the "losers," but I knew people didn't think I was very popular. I didn't have a group. Sometimes I really, really wished I had a group.

I kept writing to Daisy.

I don't have a cat. My mommy is allergic and sneezes a bunch when she gets near one. It's bad. There aren't too many pets down here. How many pets are up there??

Do you really eat clouds? (My sister told me not to ask this, but she doesn't know more than me. She only gets normal points. I get lots of class points for my group (which is purple banana)).

Do you like living up there? Is it windy?

I sometimes eat cereal out of the big mugs when everyone forgets to do dishes, and I don't say anything since sometimes I'm the reason no one did dishes. I eat out of big mugs then, and I don't think it's weird. Mine has Mystery Mouse on it! Do you like Mystery Mouse?

You like detective stuff, so I hope you've seen it.

Tell me what happens with your crime!!! I sniffed the grass but couldn't find any clues.

Please write back soon!

My name is Winifred, which isn't a good name, and my mom calls me Winnie, and my uncle calls me Freddie for fun. But I want to be "Lumin," since it means "light," and my favorite god (Apollo!!) is the god of light. I like myths, Egyptian and Greek mostly. I also like magic and TV shows about animals. I like your light!!

I hope I hear from you soon.

—Winnie

My sister told me it was too long and rambling, but I didn't know what "rambling" meant exactly, so I just ignored her. She said I needed to make real friends, and I told her that

Daisy was my real friend.
     I turned eight that year.
     I was going to find Daisy.

I didn't find Daisy. It turned out there were a lot of Daisys on the continent of Titros. I told my mom I was going write them all. She told me I could try—if I did my homework first.

They wanted me to do a lot more testing, a lot more than the other kids; I noticed. I'm not sure if they wanted me to notice or not, but I didn't think it was a secret.

Ms. Kamau kept me after school sometimes and had me take these quizzes that asked me which graphs made sense and gave me problems to solve about what kind of money I could make if I could make up a type of money. I liked the part where I made stuff up, but I was a little sick of telling them that their graphs suck.

I didn't really want to be in a separate class of just me. I had always been in the separate class, but it was a little annoying to be more separate than even the separate class. The extra lessons sometimes went long or needed me to take a test after hours. It made it hard to go to the library after school and look up the names of all the people in cloud cities. There were a lot of cloud cities at this point, and even more Daisys.

It was almost a full two months after I got that first letter when my dad picked me up from school and asked me why I had a giant book open in my lap. I sat very still, entering names into an online directory and hmm-ing. I told him that Daisy needed to know; she needed to know someone found her lantern like she wanted. I thumbed through the directory page by page. Sometimes I imagined I would recognize her, that she would look like the Daisy in my head, wearing a detective hat and holding a big, fat, white cat. Mostly I looked at old ladies and strangers in blurry CCTV photos.

I wrote a second letter in pink gel pen ink.

Dear Daisy,

Please tell me what your favorite music is (my sister says this is a good question). I like the ones where it's quiet like ocean noises and chanting, where you can't really understand the words. Sometimes they put on violin music in class, but I think voices are better.

It's pretty dark tonight. Another continent is coming overhead, but they aren't our sister one. That's what my mother said. So there are no lanterns. Just night.

It's kind of sad because I can't imagine what you're up to, like waking up in the morning and eating cereal and putting your hair up. My mom puts my hair up, but she's always too rough and pulls on my head. After hair, I put my uniform on and find my bag. My shoes are always somewhere I don't remember. Do you have uniforms up there in sky cities?

Please tell me if you have any more crimes to solve. I can help! It would be nice to be friends and send lanterns back and forth.

From,
Winnie

∞∞∞∞

It took three years before I attempted to contact Daisy in any real way. I had twelve letters by then— and some were better than others. I settled on the neatest three and some pictures of our home and family. I hoped she would like them (and that she wasn't a creep).

I put my hair up in four tidy braids for the festival that year. I had been sick with the flu the year before, and the year before that I couldn't find her lantern, no matter how hard I looked. I checked every pink one in the area, but I had a feeling Daisy had changed colors by then.

My birthday was three days earlier, but I had been thinking of the festival the entire time I was eating my cake. I was ten.

I got to wear pants to the event and even sneakers if I promised they were both all black and not even a little muddy.

I had a plan: I was going to send up the brightest airplane in the whole night sky. I had spent months working on the motor and body of the plane (it wasn't technically paper). I was in the *separate* separate class of just me most of the time. Sometimes they let me join the just-one-separate class. But not always.

They let me work on whatever project I wanted to, so long as I was working. I decided I wanted to create a tiny motor for my airplane—then it would stand out and go even higher. Ms. Kamau was fine with it. She watched me a lot or sometimes sat in the back and wrote things. Maybe she was writing letters to someone too.

My airplane said "Daisy" in giant letters on the top. The Styrofoam body was a vibrant pink, the same hue as hers all those years ago. I knew on some level that I should be *moving on* as my sister, Cami, insisted, but some things were worth seeing to the end. That's what my dad said; my mom just nodded at him. They were getting money in envelopes now. Cami told me in secret that they were for my extra classes.

They always wanted little scientists. Scientists were the ones who made continents float in the first place and solved overpopulation and the poison in the dirt. Some of the dirt was still poisoned, but the ground on the floating continents wasn't anymore, so it solved a couple problems.

I wasn't sure how I felt about all the science, but the numbers were okay if they left me alone with them for long enough. The numbers were simple, like a game I could win or a puzzle I put together myself. The plane was just another problem I could solve.

The motor came out of hours of puzzling, of numbers and sketches and drawing grids with fancy pencils that had a good grip. I told Daisy all this in my third letter: I still liked my classes, but I wished they let me do more stories about Apollo and books for fun. I was reading about Bastet now; she was an

Egyptian goddess with a cat head. I thought Daisy would like that. I included a little story I wrote myself about Apollo and Helios, about how they both wanted to ride the sun across the sky but couldn't and ended up destroying the daytime itself. I asked her about Marshmallow and what she did all day up there.

I made sure to put a streamer on the back of my airplane. Everyone loved the ones with streamers.

I made it to the festival early and avoided anyone trying to get my attention and ask me about the PISA test (*Program for Interdisciplinary Student Assessment*) and placement. I had to tell them each time that I was waiting. The Qualifier was a long way away.

I found a place in the grass behind my older sister and her new boyfriend; my dad was home that year watching Grandma, and it was just us. A little flutter spiked through my chest as I looked up. Titros was already rolling through the sky, the plastic of the hover panels reflecting off the ground and engines humming softly, a barely audible purr. Behind us, the city turned its lights off one by one.

"They do that for us," Cami's boyfriend said sweetly and tucked my sister's hair behind her ear. "They want us to see the lanterns."

I tried not to look at my sister and her boyfriend, Chege. My face was hot from watching her even giggle at one of his dumb jokes or touch his shoulder. At least *this* boyfriend was nice.

My mom was taking pictures again, standing at the very top of a craggy peak in purple lace. We waved at her as she stood with a giant smile on her face. I loved seeing her like that. I waved until my arms were tired and she still didn't see me. That was okay. Titros was almost at our doorstep and all I could do was hold my breath as the lanterns turned on one by one.

"Here it comes!" I yelled over the cheering crowds. My sister glanced over her shoulder at me and pursed her lips. She was doing that a lot more recently—pursing her lips like a coin pouch locking up. I almost missed the yelling.

"Are you going to catch another one this year, Winnie?" Chege asked me politely.

"Maybe." I sprouted a private smile. "I have a good feeling about this year."

Chege chuckled. "Good luck then, Little Mouse!" That was my sister's old nickname for me. I looked up again.

The lights rained down like falling stars one by one, little teardrops from the darkness, slowly at first until they built into a cascade of color and light. People down below whooped and wagged their hands above their heads frantically, trying to catch a good-luck lantern.

Most of them had special patterns or words of encouragement and whole phrases on the sides; many had letters within. Some letters were greetings or wishes or secrets they couldn't tell anyone else; some were just class assignments people wanted to get rid of. Some unlucky person sometimes got a prank lantern, but I preferred not to think about those fake ones.

I surveyed the sky for any pink lights, but my hopes were down. There was a high chance she switched colors by then. She didn't even know I existed in the first place. My heart sank at the thought and I bit my lip.

I still liked to chew on things, but it was mostly birthday cake–flavored gum and toothpicks now. Cami assured me neither of those things was cool.

I sat in place as people reached and reached toward the lanterns, catching them in a flurry of limbs and laughter. I watched as Chege jogged purposefully to one with a bright, blood-red heart in the center. My sister squealed as he caught it and presented it to her. I had to look away again and stuck my tongue out like I could spit out the image of it.

The lanterns dangled and dipped, gifted to the waiting ground-dwellers. This wasn't what I was waiting for, though. I sat with my back completely straight and eyes focused on the far corner of the festival. My chest tightened with the force of an angry bear trap. A cannon blast pierced the air, and voices raised euphorically with it.

"There it goes!" I sprang to my feet. My sister was busy embracing her boyfriend, and I didn't pause to tell them I was going. I simply took off. I cut a path toward the floating continent, keeping my eyes up. The stream of little paper planes arched in the air, a curved river overhead.

I sprinted, chasing the perfect arch of planes as far as I could. Eyes searching and straining, I spotted a stark white streamer just in time: *Daisy!* It said, *Daisy!* It was well above the others.

I could only pray she saw it. The people were just waving outlines on the island, unreal, wiggling stick figures with one voice and one blobby body. I couldn't even imagine what Daisy looked like, what her last name was, what she thought about when she went to bed.

I watched as outstretched shadow fingers caught the little planes one by one. My plane disappeared into the above.

Catch it.

I willed, praying to something indistinct and nameless, something that must make the lanterns float in the first place.

Please, catch it.

I gave chase until I was breathless and sweating out of every pore from the thick summer air; my chest heaved, and I tried to see something that wasn't there. I imagined her plucking the airplane from the sky, cradling it, and discovering my letters fixed snugly into the center crevice. I imagined she was relieved—someone had gotten her lantern all that time ago and it meant something.

I prayed.

I was eleven. Eleven and seventy-two days.

Preliminary tests were coming up fast and furious now. For the first time, I was almost struggling in school and wished I was outside doing anything else.

My sister was learning to drive, and my mom was claiming the upstairs storage area for a dark room. She was developing photographs for real now. Most of them she bunched up and threw away in the big garbage bins outside with stony-faced silence. There was one, though, a toddler with their little fists up in the air, shrieking happily as the lantern lights reflected off their chubby cheeks. I didn't know what she saw in that one, but she kept looking.

My father was trying to get a hot tub for the backyard. It was a very long process that I thought was taking much longer than strictly necessary. My dad was always fixing something—fixing and adding and taking his dinner in the garage now. The hot tub was being bought from the stipends the government sent.

They weren't talking to me like they used to. I wished terribly to talk to somebody, but even when I was around the other kids, it was like my tongue was made of moon rocks. There were names written on the board, stacked neatly one by one with tally marks by their side.

My name was always at the top.

I closed my eyes every night and tried to think about what Daisy was doing, what I would tell her if we could talk. I might lie a little bit. I wouldn't tell her about wanting to talk to the others or how my mom didn't fix my hair like she used to or any of my rankings.

It was a nice fantasy.

It was the end of summer. I had just grown out of my old plaid uniform and into a new one with a bow in front and inside pockets. I ran back and forth across the living room, looking for it.

"Mom," I called to the upstairs, "have you seen my new jacket?"

My sister's pop-y "getting-ready" music answered me instead, and I turned around in useless circles.

"Ugh!" I ran back across to the closet and started riffling

through my dad's tweed jackets he wore for conferences and "chardonnay" nights. I found nothing but moths hidden in the corners.

I was running back toward the kitchen when a chat icon lit up on the family computer. The touch screen was fixed to the wall behind a broad, official-looking glass. A little, white notification pinged brightly in the corner. I frowned at it for a moment before passing by.

Probably for my sister, I noted briefly, assuming it was some assignment from a classmate or friend wanting to go to the mall this weekend. My jacket was hidden at the bottom of a laundry basket, and I had to hurry out the door with only a slice of toast in my mouth.

The day went by like every other: they let me do independent study for an hour, always building something. I didn't mind building things, but the joy of it was kind of soured after my motor didn't make any difference at the festival.

All my hard work, and it didn't amount to anything.

I poked and prodded at the electronic bits of a cube that could show you the weather of any place on Earth if you entered a location and turned it over. It was as pretty as it was superfluous. We already had weather apps. I brought the cube to my second class. It was called "guided study" technically and was already in progress. This one had five other students in it, but none of them looked at me when I came in the door.

The teacher waved a hand in my direction, and I settled into my chair at the front. Then I slipped my phone out of my pocket to check the time. There was a chat ping in the corner of my screen.

I blinked at it a couple times. A family chat notification was one thing—I blinked again—but this meant it was for me! I sat up straight in my chair and made sure no one was paying attention. My neighbor, Ash, was consumed in her robotics project and the teacher was helping Tumanai.

I quickly poked at the ping to see where the message was from, and my eyes went wide. *From: DA.* DA from a global satellite address in the middle of the Pacific.

My heart leaped into my throat. *That has to be a floating continent.* It had to be her.

I thrust my hand in the air.

"Can I go to the bathroom?" I almost shouted. The entire class turned toward me, but I stopped caring what they thought almost a year ago. I knew for a fact they were the ones who threw all my pencils out the window right before the PISA 1 practice test.

My teacher adjusted her glasses. "What's that, Miss Otiena?"

I scrunched my nose up and made a split-second decision. School was too suffocating for this, for Daisy's first words. "I need to go home."

"You just said bathroom," Ash hissed at me. I made a face at her.

"I feel awful." I slumped down on my desk, and my teacher adjusted her glasses again.

Brief haggling ensued, but I had never asked to be excused before, never asked for any favors or even assignment extensions. She had no choice but to believe me. She didn't even bother calling my parents. I was eleven now. And separate.

I ran home with my pulse throbbing in my wrist and eyes wide. It could be a false alarm. It could be a prank. It could be that I had finally lost it.

I rushed through the front door, kicked off my shoes, and darted toward the linen closet. I grabbed sheets and a blanket, moving to drape them between the rocking chair and couch. An impromptu fort. I crawled into the soft depths and huddled in the dark.

The little light of my phone glowed on my face. I wiped down my sweaty palms, and my fingers trembled as I pushed the chat button.

A message dinged up immediately.

"Hello! This is Daisy." My computer offered to read it out loud for me. I scrambled to decline. I closed the program immediately, taking deep, heaving breaths.

"She's here," I cried as I buried my smiling face in my arms. "She's here, she's here!" I couldn't help it. I had been waiting. Daisy. Daisy Ayim, it said.

I bit my lip and wished I had something to chew through. I had her name, her whole name. And she knew I was someone.

I almost started to dance. *She got my plane!* The world was somehow brighter and more in-focus than it ever had been before.

It took several more minutes before I could even think about opening the chat program again. My thoughts whirled around, caught in a tumble cycle of the washing machine in my head. Some part of me hadn't thought this would ever work.

What will I fantasize about after this? I gulped. *What if I make it bad?*

I took deep, rattling breaths. I had worked for this. I couldn't keep Daisy waiting. I opened her messages again.

Sent: 7:46 a.m.

DA: Hello, Winnie!

Compared to her first letter, there were a lot less exclamation points.

DA: I'm sorry it took me so long to respond. I had to beg my parents to believe this was real.

DA: but . . . it looked real!

DA: You were seven when you got my lantern? That's so embarrassing. I barely remember what I wrote. But . . . thank you. I was pretty excited when I saw an entire plane with my name on it. I almost lost it!

DA: I don't know what I'm writing, sorry

DA: Anyway, my name is Daisy Ayim. I'm turning thirteen later this month :). Marshmallow passed away when I was nine sadly. :(As for your questions . . .

DA: Things I like: thriller movies, any music that isn't country, and horses, though I've never seen one. I don't like game shows, since they seem so fake. I don't really want to be a detective anymore.

My mouth fell open as I read. Daisy had written back. Daisy had responded a lot. She was around my age. She liked horses; she didn't like game shows! She was a real person, not something I made up.

I put my phone down and rolled onto my back. I started tracing the lines of Titros I could remember, doodling its shape with my fingers on the bed sheet and dreaming.

"Daisy," I mouthed the word. I didn't know what to say back.

∞∞∞

I really didn't know what to say to her. I figured it would come to me. I slept on it. But it didn't come—not the next day or the day after that.

Daisy kept messaging me.

Sent 5:58 p.m.

DA: Hey, I'm sorry if I said anything weird.

DA: I hope I got the right number. Maybe you lost your phone or you're grounded and your parents took it from you. :(

DA: That sometimes happens to me. It sucks. I'm locked up in my room right now. I don't know what my mom's problem is.

DA: >:(

DA: It's always this or that. I don't feel like a "trouble-maker" or whatever, but every detention makes her freak the H out. It's not even big stuff—detention for running in the halls, detention for talking in class, detention for writing my essay the RIGHT way, ugh.

DA: I mean, everyone knows that the Fifth War was started because leaders had cotton stuffed in their ears and HUUUGE frickin' egos.

DA: It's not news! Mr. V. just has some serious hang-ups.

DA: Anyway … I'm sorry if I said anything to offend you.

DA: I think …

DA: I think that plane is the sweetest thing anyone's ever done for me.

DA: Good night, Winnie.

That was the second day. I read her messages over breaks, over dinner, smiling down at my lap as my father tried to ask me about my studies and my sister rolled her eyes. I read it before bed, first once, and then twenty times.

I liked Daisy Ayim.

I needed to say something cool to her.

Sent 4:13 p.m.

DA: Day three!

DA: I'm still freaking grounded. It sucks so hard.

DA: Do you ever get grounded? I hope you are right now.

DA: Oh dang, that sounds bad. I just mean I hope you message me. The computer says this is the right address. Winnie Otiena, right? That's what your letters said.

Sent 6:42 p.m.

DA: Who do you think was the most handsome member of the imperial Russian dynasty? I'm doing a history project.

DA: The title is "Hottie or Romanov-notty?" It's a think piece.

Sent 7:01 p.m.

DA: I got double grounded! My mother must not agree that Ivan the Terrible was a notty.

DA: ...

DA: This is probably why you aren't messaging me back, isn't it?

My heart sank when I read that. I needed to say something. I needed to tell her that I thought she was funny, cool, that I thought we'd have fun if we went to school together. My head fell, hitting the desk and bouncing. I sighed into the wood.

She probably wouldn't have been in my classes if we were in school together. She probably wouldn't have sat with me at lunch. I squeezed my eyes shut tight and tried to formulate anything to say that might interest her. Anything at all. The words didn't come to me.

Daisy kept going.

Sent 8:11 a.m.

DA: Here's a cute picture of a dog:
[FILE PICTURE]

DA: Does this make me normal? I honestly don't want you to think I'm that weird.

DA: Here's a list of my favorite members of V-W in order of best hair to worst personality:
[FILE PICTURE]

Daisy was bored and interesting, and I was interested and boring. I couldn't figure out how to bridge that gap and get over myself. I was stuck in myself.

It would be months before the next festival.

Daisy kept writing.

∞∞∞

She hated asparagus and loved salty things, ranging from fried chips to peanuts right out of the jar. She started listening to punk rock in middle school out of spite and now she was wholly dedicated to the band Summer of the Damned and religiously cutting up her jackets. She loved the color gray, the type that was almost silver. She wanted to paint her whole room that color, but her mom wouldn't let her.

She didn't have any siblings, but she swore her friend Kiki was close enough.

Her parents apparently circled her like vultures, sniffing for problems.

It was a month before the next festival, and I was working harder than I had ever worked before. I had a new project coursing through my veins and urging me to keep my eyes open and open and open. My fingers moved ceaselessly over worksheets and little, tiny gears.

It was ten days until the festival.

I spent a lot of nights memorizing my ceiling at that point. It wasn't that I didn't like sleep; it felt more like I was forgetting how. The room smelled of cut summer grass and midnight sprinklers *chita-chita-chit-chit-ing* somewhere in the neighborhood. My windows were jammed open, and the bedside clock blinked: one in the morning, one thirty, two.

I stared over my room unseeingly, going over numbers in my head and recent test scores. My parents would get more stipends the higher I reached, and the higher I reached, the more it meant. And then the next step: the Qualifier.

I didn't want to think about the Qualifier.

My phone pinged. I turned it over as quickly as I could.

Sent 2:27 a.m.

DA: Sometimes I feel like nothing I do will be good enough for her.

DA: I couldn't even buy birthday flowers for her right. She's "allergic" to that type of tulip, apparently.

DA: It doesn't matter if I try.

DA: None of it makes her happy. Do you ever worry about that, Winnie?

DA: That you'll never be good enough?

DA: Winnie?

I held the phone close to my chest and imagined the words I would write back to her if I could.

WO: I feel that way sometimes, Daisy. I think it's normal.

WO: I think you're the best thing that's happened to me. Please don't think that about yourself. You don't have to be good enough.

WO: Everything about you

WO: is good.

I didn't write that.

I wrapped my fingers around my phone, right up against my thumping heart, and fell asleep like that.

∞∞∞

Daisy went quiet after that message. I tried not to let it bother me. I was busy enough as it was—and this had to be perfect. I couldn't be distracted, and I feared any more worries might weigh me down like a capsizing ship. That perhaps if I stopped, I might never start again.

I focused on collecting all my responses to Daisy from the last couple months. The first one was an apology. It was on flower paper and had at least five crying emojis throughout. The paper read briefly:

Hey, Daisy,

I'm so so so sorry I didn't message back yet. I wanted to say something cool! But I waited too long and the pressure kept building up! I'm so sorry. I know this isn't cool either.

—Winnie

If Daisy stopped messaging me after that, then that's how it would be. But I had to clear the air, tell her how I felt. I had to try again.

I turned twelve that year; my birthday party was an airless, sterile thing with store-bought cake and quiet conversation. I counted down the hours until the more important event.

The festival burst as it always did, stuffed with dazzling noise and lights, the bottom of the jagged hills rippling with warm bodies and tempting scents of fried bananas and turkey legs. I crept through it as a wisp, reaching a modest white building at the very back corner and letting myself inside. The launch prep room was compact and simple; a single table and registry sat at the back. It was empty, except for a security camera on the ceiling. Air conditioning coughed through the vents but sweat trickled down my shoulder blades anyway as I cradled a large white plane. It was heavy in my hands—maybe too heavy—and it made me chew my bottom lip like a piece of rubber.

I glanced out the huge windows just in time to see our sister continent come sweeping across the horizon, bleeding into the night and eating up half the sky. My mouth went dry and tasteless. I quickly looked back down to my twitching hands and foam plane. *Is it ready?* A bell like a fire alarm went off— launch would be soon. I hunched over to check my engine's batteries, the fuse, the timer, the release switch.

There were five typed letters stuffed into the fat airplane. I hoped they stayed fixed in there after everything. My jaw hurt from clenching it. A second bell rang. I knocked on the far door and a middle-aged woman in a long green dress and a visor looked back at me. "I know this is late . . ." I offered weakly and, with nothing left, handed her my plane.

The festival master examined it skeptically for a moment.

"What's this?" She pointed at the little propeller on the back. "Does it go?"

"It goes." I stood up straight and pushed on, "It's on a

timer. It should start right at the launch hour."

The little motor and basket hitched on its back were both technically not allowed. The entire thing was off model for that matter—it wasn't even paper. She shrugged, smiling in a knowing way, though I had no idea what she could possibly know. She placed my plane into a chute leading outside. "Just in time."

I exhaled.

My phone trembled in my cracked, dry hands, and I stumbled back outside. The lanterns had already fallen; only the planes were left. I squeezed my phone, typing as fast as I could before my thoughts could catch up to me and drag me back into the dark waters of stasis.

Sent 10:31 p.m.

WO: Daisy, look up!

I didn't know where I found the courage, or if I found it at all, but my fingers were flying.

WO: Please look up!

A blast of air tickled the back of my neck, and the sound of wind chimes and the shout of a cannon erupted as thousands of little airplanes were pushed high into the sky. Shot toward the continent and waiting crowds.

My plane was slightly higher than the others. I saw the mechanisms clicking together in my mind's eye, working away to ignite the end of the trailing string. Right on cue, a spark ate its way up the fuse toward the waiting basket. The little plane let out a series of pops and crackles. The colors fizzled and boomed, shooting into the air and twisting into large, glittering letters.

DAISY!

I wrote the letters in curling fireworks that filled the sky. I wished I had more to say, but the glowing "Daisy" hung in the air with a brash, unapologetic vibrance.

I exhaled, hoping the rest of the plane made it safely to the continent after the fireworks released. I hoped she looked up.

I petered to a slow stop, taking a moment to sag to my knees and flop over on the grass, looking up blankly. Crowds churned around me, and the smell of nearby buttered popcorn soothed my frayed nerves. My mother was nowhere to be seen. My father was putting together our new hover car somewhere. My sister was eating ice cream with her friends and showing off a new tattoo.

I was lying on my back, looking up, panting, phone clutched in my fingers.

I told myself I didn't care if she messaged back after that, but my phone hung empty and quiet next to me. Hot pin pricks stung at the corners of my eyes and a strangled feeling bubbled up in waves that bound me to the ground.

She had every right to be mad. I held the phone tighter. I told myself she never had to talk to me again. It was only right.

Ping.

I let the stress tears roll down my cheeks before wiping at them and twisting over to open the chat program.

Sent 9:03 p.m.

DA: aaaaaaaaaaaaaaaaaaaaaaaaaahh
DA: I DIDN'T KNOW YOU GOT MY MESSAGES
DA: aaaaaaaaaaaaaaaaaaaaaahhhhhh

A smiled consumed my face from the inside out. I forced myself to move again.

WO: Don't worry about it.
WO: Hi, my name is Winifred Otiena. I am twelve. I still like the color pink and think that your detective business would have been wonderful.

51

WO: I've seen a horse but think they're a little too big.
WO: And thank you.
WO: Thank you so much for messaging me.
DA: You've been reading this crap??
WO: Please don't stop.
WO: I'm not great with words, but I like yours.
DA: Well . . . hi.
WO: Hello.

Several minutes passed. I looked at the screen with a panic rising like a tide. I stepped harshly on the brakes.

WO: How was your day?

I jabbed my fingers against the screen and sent with a furious force. My whole being vibrated as her typing bubbles sprang up.

DA: Wait.
DA: Prove you're a real person.
WO: How?
DA: Got a picture?

It felt like an out-of-body experience to take a picture of my sweaty face surrounded by grass and hair loose in the dirt. I was wearing a blank tank top and raggedy jeans. Luckily, I didn't have to include those.

[PICTURE SENT]
DA: Aaaaaaaaahh
DA: You're real real!
WO: Real real.

We started to talk. It was touch and go at first. I still had to hide my face sometimes and bully my circle-thoughts into a corner, but Daisy filled in the gaps with her chatter. And we began.

∞∞∞

I was thirteen. I was writing a girl on a floating island. The girl on the island was writing me back. I received a lantern that year with my name on it. "Winnie" written in blue and white and glittery accents that caught the eye. A tiny firework was inside.

And there was a note: *Not quite the same as yours! But you might like this one. Ha ha, don't blow your fingers off!*

The tiny firework erupted yellow and orange. It smelled like peaches and citrus oranges. I set it off by myself in my back-yard and watched the lights well past when they stopped burst-ing.

We discussed video chatting, but I kept saying I had a cold. I kept getting colds like that each time it was brought up. Nonetheless, I told her that year: you're my favorite person I've ever talked to. She told me she'd blow my mind with a lantern one of these days, that it would be her pleasure.

∞∞∞

I was fourteen. I sent Daisy an airplane with origami swans on the top. Daisy sent me a lantern with five clues inside. Each clue built up to the answer for an elaborate murder mystery story on the back of a mac-and-cheese box they only had on Titros.

I solved it in two hours, but I didn't tell her that. She told me she'd make a better criminal now than a detective anyway.

I was fifteen.

Daisy sent me a lantern that year with wings on it, wings and cotton-fluff floating clouds around the base. It held pages of shredded poetry each with a different line from artists ranging from Homer to Sappho to the new band she liked called Wildfire Tourists. I caught it and took a selfie with the last bits of paper and orange glow.

We talked for the whole night.

∞∞∞

I was sixteen and messaging Daisy every moment my hands weren't busy. Daisy was on her third suspension, and I was spending less and less time at home or in bed. We had a new house, new neighborhood. We celebrated my sister leaving for college.

I missed her terribly. My parents were just glad she didn't keep extending her "gap year."

I was more grateful than ever for someone else to talk to.

Daisy sent me a lantern with CGI walls and a moving picture on each side. One was of kittens, and the next of clouds, and the third of fireworks. The last one was of roses, blooming and blooming in slow motion. She sent me chocolates inside that tasted like bourbon and orange sugar. She said she wanted to taste real bourbon one day, and I told her I wanted to own a real kitten. She sent me a heart back.

I went through my second growth spurt and still barely reached five foot two.

I sent Daisy an airplane with flowers from the ground: daisies and poppies. She said there weren't any poppies up there. She put them on her bedside table and sent me pictures of them every morning until they wilted.

A man in a suit visited me. My mom let him in the front door, and he shook my hand like I wasn't breaking out on my forehead and wearing a cartoon mouse T-shirt. He asked me how my Qualifier prep classes were going and if I needed anything. He was from the WG, a real government man. My mother gave him the good tea before they all sat down around the kitchen table. I perched on a stool, shaking my head sometimes and not contributing to the discussion of whatever *the future* held for me.

∞∞∞∞

I was seventeen.

Daisy sent me a lantern that was red walls and silk insides. The outside was decorated with pressed flowers and smelled like her perfume. I blushed and sent her a plane that played lyrical ballads and held a simple silver bracelet. I asked her if she would wear it. She said she already had it super-glued on.

I was tired, though perhaps *tired* was more of a state of being than an adjective by then. My days were a blurry thread with no end and no beginning, sluggish and scattered as an abstract painting with numbers and figures floating through my head. The graphs had gotten more complicated, and I was getting worse at stacking myself upright and answering.

I kept getting the same message from Daisy, over and over.

DA: Where do you go after you "qualify"?
WO: I don't know.
DA: Find out!
WO: That's classified. The WG only shows you a little pamphlet and a peek at the paycheck.
DA: :/
DA: What exactly do you qualify for?
WO: I dunno.
WO: The world?
DA: :/

∞∞∞∞

I was almost eighteen.

I felt the age creeping up on me like a witch about to curse my soul and suck it out of my body with a straw. I told Daisy about that and she told me she would be the only witch in my life, promise. She was already nineteen. She got a temporary job at a shoe store.

I didn't know what to tell her. She sent me snaps of the concerts she went to and her guitar practice with a shark-tooth guitar pick. I showed her my tired, puffy face in return.

The Qualifier was at the end of spring. It was five days long with a different subject each day: three hours, a lunch break, and then two more hours. I broke out in nervous hives days before, hunching over unreadable letters with a sickness with no name. Daisy messaged me the day before.

DA: Botch the test.

WO: I can't. They'll know. They already know what I can do.

DA: ... don't go.

WO: You can't say that.

DA: Don't go! You don't know where they're taking you.

WO: Humanity's brightest. They're gathering us.

WO: It's how we got the floating cities ... the World Government, everything. They need me.

DA: They don't need you!!! Not all of you, at least, 'cause that's what you're giving them, Winnie.

DA: Don't go.

WO: Wait

WO: for me

I started shaking. Did I really have to go? Did I want to go? My parents barely spoke in our sprawling new house. My sister was trying to fail gracefully out of an expensive private college. I had nightmares of hands and timers every night, the hives spread, and I was too tired to cry.

I took the test. Five days, with a different subject each day: three hours, and then a break for lunch and two more hours. My hands shook from the elbows down, and my wrists ached until the last day, when they melted into numb, blocky nothingness. I stacked the completed mountain of white paper on a government man's desk, and I waited for relief. I found only more blocky nothingness instead.

I didn't open the WG letter when it came, fat, gold-sealed, and sitting on our doorstep like a wrapped present. My parents hung the contents on the wall above the family computer. My mom turned and smiled. "Three more months, Winnie, and then you're there," she said without looking at me. "Everything you've worked for."

"We're so proud of you," my father added, but I didn't hear him.

I was going to solve all of humanity's problems, solve them all somewhere I didn't know with people who only knew me through score cards. Somewhere with no location on the maps or anyone I knew of that came back from it. A half-packed suitcase sat on my bed, filled with socks, baggy shorts, notebooks, threadbare T-shirts, and a black suit jacket with silk pockets.

Daisy sent me three articles.

DA: READ. THIS.
[LINK RECEIVED]
DA: Read them right now, Winnie.
[LINK RECEIVED]
[LINK RECEIVED]

I wasn't sure I wanted to. I needed to finish packing. I had spent weeks trying to get up the energy to fold another pair of pants. I clicked on them anyway, my stomach already cramping at the headlines.

Activist Mother Protests Qualifiers: Claims She Hasn't Seen Her Son in Years

Pushing Past the Limits for Brilliance: World Government Releasing Exclusive Files on How They Give Our Brightest Minds an Edge

A Method to the Madness: Schools Isolating Top Students for Results

I clicked on the last one.

Does competition and strategic isolation help young minds bloom? One investigation says that the next crisis may well be averted through grooming the next generation.
But at what cost?
Specialized teachers are allegedly taught to pick out the brightest and set their peers at odds with them. Experts claim that cultivating self-reliance and resilience are key to unlocking full potential. One such teacher gave the Weekly Wordwise a behind-the-scenes glance into the method behind "Strategic Isolation."

I closed the article. I had seen enough. I went back to my workshop that night, or maybe it was morning by then. I started building again. I started bruising my fingers on nuts and bolts, forming something made of scrap metal and fairy tales.

I broke into our old hover car and took out the resistors.

I borrowed the reflectors from my neighbor's toolshed and sun plates from the community garden green room.

I stopped going to class, to meetings, to dinner. No one intervened. I had already qualified.

The days dripped by like melting candlewax down the body of a shrinking candle.

Daisy prompted us to video chat, and for once I didn't say no. Some of my worries about messing this all up had fried during the endless test. It was time to see each other. I had been putting it off in the way you put off a warm bath or getting on a roller coaster with no safety gear. There were thirteen days until the festival.

I arrived home early in the afternoon, wearing my workshop overalls and ink on my fingertips. I never thought about being "cute." I was what I was. My body carried me to class and back home. It didn't need to be anything else. I spent an hour twisting my hair up into something approximately elegant. I pinched my cheeks and slathered on lip gloss, practicing tilting my chin up confidently in the mirror. I had never thought about being cute, and I suddenly very much wanted to be cute. I sat in front of my wall computer in my room, tilting, pinching, looking.

An image buzzed to life before me before I could dive under my desk or find another Winnie somewhere with better teeth and words that didn't buck and shy away from her at every turn.

"Oh," I breathed softly. Daisy appeared like a mirage.

She had a round face and an infinitely wide smile, beautifully bright-eyed and dark-skinned as me, lovely as a dream. Daisy had shoulder-length hair that crowned her face in a halo of tight curls where she was the sun in the middle. She had a silver septum piercing in her nose and heavy eyeliner that matched her dark jacket, and it was everything I imagined.

I touched the screen lightly, and she grinned back at me. "So"—she made a hiccup of noise—"where is my postcard from earth?"

I smiled back. "Wait for it."

I was almost done.

∞∞∞

The warm night clothed me in a tight wrapping, and I shook slightly in the careless summer breeze. I didn't know if they were watching. The WG had cameras everywhere, but perhaps they thought I was going to fail.

I knew the reflectors would only last a couple minutes. I knew the hover engine might barely hold me up. I swallowed thickly. *Maybe she won't want to see me after the first day. Maybe I'll ruin it.*

I knew I would miss my parents, but I wouldn't miss the headaches, the tests, the threat of tomorrow, the choking compressor on my chest set to burst. I wouldn't miss the nights when I did manage to sleep and dreamed of nothing but dead-end mazes and voices screeching at me from every side to save them.

I perched on the edge of the gulch, gaping and huge across the otherwise flat plains. This was the place where they first scooped out the earth, purified it, and made it capable of bearing life again. Then they pushed it lovingly into the sky, past the choking black clouds and toward something you could make wishes on.

Trees returned to the gulch, tentative and lunging for sun with a vengeful hunger; the saplings had all come from the floating continents first, though.

I reached up and closed my eyes, inhaling deeply as the wind licked my feverish face. It felt like forever ago that I stood here and chased a small pink lantern around in circles. I trembled and opened my eyes just as the first colors of glowing light came softly floating down from Titros.

I engaged the hover transistors of my wings. My shoulders tensed and the machine rattled jarringly against my spine.

"Daisy." I tried to make her out in the crowd on the land above, but I couldn't. "Daisy."

I prayed again, but it was different now, not pleading or nameless. Just simple: *Take me away.*

I held my breath as my feet lightly, slowly stopped bearing my weight, and I touched off the earth in a single, slender step. I hung in the air just above the tips of the grass. The motor I had been developing since I was nine vibrated with life, fury, terror. I pushed off from the earth.

My hover wings held me up, and I instructed my thrusters to engage. Their voice drummed like a battle cry and energy spiked. With a jerk I hurtled toward Titros, to the shiny black honeycomb sky and away from the eyes of the World Government. Titros belonged to itself.

I reached my hands out, temples pounding, and everything became a blur of light and sound as I drove through the wind, up and up and up.

"Daisy!" My voice was hoarse and almost gone. I was afraid I would be shot down. That I would be chased and punished and told I had failed them. All of them.

I saw the edge of the continent like the drop-off of the known universe and reached for the very bottom of the first panel. Gasping, voices called from far below, yelling just loud enough for me to hear.

"Hey, girl!"

"Who is that?"

"What is she doing...?"

"What's that on her back?"

"Look at the smoke! She's going to fall!"

I glanced behind me. A sliver of smoke trailed above my head, just as promised.

The ignition stuttered. A cough came from the engine, and wrenching fear shot through my gut. My homemade wings sputtered. The world was popping and whirring all around me. The air rushed through my ears, through my hair. I gasped. *No.*

One last burst launched me inches from the bottom of the continent's panels, and then the vibration against my spine stopped altogether. Color drained from the fabric of the world and time slowed.

My fingers grasped at nothing, and my ears rang with the coming fall.

"Winnie!" A hand surged forward, wrapping around my wrist and yanking.

"Daisy!" I cried out as a joy beyond joy took hold and heat surged throughout my whole body from where she touched me. "There you are."

I was pulled into Titros, a hole in the sky that sucked me up. Daisy yanked and dragged until I tumbled into the dark inner bowels of the continent. She wrapped her arms around me, and I fell into the depths.

Voices were still calling out, perhaps demanding that I come back or mend the planet or save them all. The panel closed behind me. I took a single shaking breath before Daisy pulled me tighter to her chest, chasing away every thought I ever had.

"You made it." She laughed against my damp skin. "Took you long enough."

All I could do was nod, finding my voice from some dust that settled within. "Yeah," I sighed the word. "Couldn't stay away."

Smiling, she put her hands on my shoulders and our eyes met in the dimness. "Nice flying."

My lips twitched up. "Nice catch."

She drew forward, looking at me in a way I had never been looked at before. Then she grinned impishly. "It was, wasn't it? I must be good at first impressions."

I wet my lips. "It's not over yet." I touched her face and whispered, "So, hello, Daisy Ayim. I'm Winnie Otiena. It's nice to make your acquaintance."

She shook lightly, a breath away, a hair away. "Acquaintances, huh?" She leaned the rest of the way forward, crossing galaxies. "That's a lot to live up to." Our gaze held. "But I'll try."

We came together, something that tore away all the sloppy little stitches that held me together for so long, spilling out red and white and sunburnt heat. The kiss was soft and warm and tumbling through me like river rapids.

I held her close, and we kissed in the dark for a very long moment as a weightlessness swooped and ballooned in my chest. I was invincible—I was everything, and nothing. We opened our eyes slowly and tapped our foreheads together, breathing in time with each other.

"This is my favorite thing you've sent," she whispered, a light dancing in her gaze.

I grinned. "No returns."

We came together again.

The Bog Hag

I was a little over four hundred years old when she arrived. Young for the ages, but old for what I used to be.

I felt the vibrations before I saw her: dainty feet, an uneven tilt to her steps, sloppy, like pancakes hitting a hot skillet and splattering. I bet my last five teeth that she was a late walker, late to crawl, late to lumber across my path. I curled my lips back and grinned wildly; of course, something like her gait wouldn't matter much after this.

She took a couple steps across the wooden planks, barefoot—like she was tempting me without a prayer to her name—and then stopped. I waited for another minute for those prime pale ankles to come within my reach, but she just stood there.

I peeked quietly out of my hole and scowled; a head was hanging down over the edge of the railing. Rivers of lank blond hair cascaded toward the water accompanied by a small face, frowning mouth, cherry nose, and sharp eyes.

Her eyes were pale green and sat under large expressive eyebrows, thick and rounded things—like fat caterpillars.

Her mouth quirked to the side and her small features bunched up. I snorted loudly. She was wickedly beautiful; I would've eaten her right then and there if she wasn't looking at me with the type of directness only arrogance can summon.

I presented my darkened teeth to her, spreading my long, thin fingers out and leaning into the dim light as the muddy water parted around me.

"Well, well, well," I said as I flexed my fingers and coated my words with syrupy sweetness, "they really do serve themselves up on a platter these days."

I licked my lips rapaciously.

The young woman tilted her head to the side, and her golden rivers of hair rippled in place. She observed me from upside down. "I don't think so," she finally spoke and then flashed me her fine fingers, chubby and small to match her figure. One golden rose ring shone from her pointer finger, and I hissed.

"Royal brat."

She shrugged and finally stood up properly to peer down at me. "Come out," she said.

I scowled. "You may have immunity, but I don't take orders. You are all temporary." I squatted down in the sludge and grumbled. "I am the trees and wind, the dark of the waters. You will pass. I will not."

"Yeah, yeah." She flicked her wrist. "I just wanna see."

My eyes turned to slits. "What the inside of my belly looks like? I'd be happy to accommodate."

She could have only been around eighteen, young, blithe, angry about something I couldn't guess at.

She cushioned her chin on her folded arms and blinked down. "I wish I looked like you."

I made a face, more of one than usual. "The little girl wants the devil under her skin. How special."

The girl rolled her eyes in a magnificent circle. "I'm not little," she said loudly, "and you know what I mean."

I was overtaken by a strange puzzlement with the girl. "What's your name, little bird?"

She growled. "Not. Little," she repeated. "I'm almost twenty and I'm not dumb enough to give my name to a witch."

I shrugged. "It seemed like you were."

"Ugh." She leaned over the railing. "I wish all I had to do was sit under a bridge and tease strangers. And my mom says *I'm* the ungrateful one."

"Tease and then eat them," I said in an exasperated tone.

"You're leaving out the most important part."

She hummed lowly. "What do people taste like?"

I smacked my lips together. "Like juicy, juicy pig meat, but more tender."

She laughed with a rich, full sound. "Liar."

I frowned at her. "Don't you have places to be? You are a royal."

She scrunched her face up and pushed her loose blond hair back. "Why do you think I'm here? I'm trying *not* to have things to do."

I looked her up and down. "I don't remember being invited to the birth of such a brat," I commented dryly. "Is that Hessia family spurning me again?"

She sighed loudly. "Nah." The girl reached into her pocket and flashed another ring in my direction; this one was an ornate blue sparrow. "I'm not from here."

"Ah." I mulled that over for a second. "It's a good thing they already extended their immunity to you. Just remember to invite me to the wedding or I'll—"

"Or you'll unleash the gale-force winds and raise the water and curse our children. I've heard."

I grimaced and peeled my lips back from my teeth. "Do they not have manners where you're from?" I asked mildly. "Or are you simply in the mood to push your luck?"

I wandered farther out of my tunnel. The pale sunlight bathed my earthy hair, covered in twigs and dirt and the wiggling life. One bird pecked away for earthworms there. The girl stiffened as she examined me, taking in my puffy green skin, my wrecked knuckles, my parched mouth, the hunch of my back, and my long mud-caked gown. I smiled so widely I think I almost cracked my face in half.

She placed her chin on her arms again. "I'm not here to have manners," she said lowly. "You don't have any, as I can tell. Why should I?" She sighed. "What's this bargain with the devil again?"

I shook my head. "Too high a price," I muttered quietly

and tilted my chin upward, eyes glowing ember yellow and long nose catching the light. I was now fully exposed in the swampy waters. "Are you sure you still want to look like me, lovely bird?"

She raised her eyebrows. "Oh yes," she said simply. "Who wouldn't?" She smiled an uncomplicated smile and then turned around. "Prince Jace will probably send out the dogs if I am gone any longer, but"—she pushed her hair aside and looked over her shoulder—"I'm Tuck."

"Tuck." I rolled the name around on my tongue and tried to consume the vowels and suck the marrow out of the consonants. My expression soured.

"Not my real name, obviously," she said with a smirk, "but everyone calls me that. Or used to."

I was still gnashing on something I couldn't quite chew. "Fascinating," I said dryly and swept into a mock bow. "Lady Tuck then."

She waved. "They told me there was a powerful bog hag in these parts." She examined me. "It was nice to meet you."

Now she has manners, I noted bitterly.

The strange girl turned around and started walking. I grinned after her and imagined sinking my teeth around her pale throat, letting the red droplets spill out and color my muddy brown waters. I blinked a couple times and then grumbled about the royals; they could always do more to me, it seemed, including being nuisances.

Tuck's unsteady footsteps disappeared without a trace, and I closed my eyes and sank into the warm, earthy waters again.

I was around four hundred at the time . . . young for the steady trees and arching rivers, old for what I used to be.

"On a scale of one to ten, how clever do you actually find fairies?"

Tuck was sitting at the edge of the water, pale blue skirts crumpled under her and feet narrowly close to the lapping pond.

I sighed loudly in exasperation. "Go home, little birdie." I waved my hand in the air. "Your presence isn't requested here."

She glanced up mildly. "That isn't even a proper answer. Are centaurs truly as health obsessed as they say? My uncle met one, and he said all the poor fellow could talk about was his kneecaps and the next plague. A right hypochondriac."

My left eyebrow twitched. "Why don't you go ask one?"

Tuck reclined backward into the dappled sunlight. "Does it look like I know many Mythics? I'm asking *you*," she said loudly,

I glowered over at her. "You must have books," I said with a sneer. "Rooms full of them I hear, houses full."

Tuck crossed her arms over her chest. "And what would the court say? That's what Matilda would remind me. The future queen burying herself in otherworldly material." Tuck snorted noisily. "I would never get away with it."

"But you get away with conversing with a bog hag?" I reminded her pointedly, mostly so I could return to my hunting. "How progressive."

She cracked an almost-smile. "Oh, yes, they call it a glorious new diplomatic mission." She lifted her chin up proudly. "One only for the foreign queen, of course. Taking up friendship with the local terrors."

I scoffed. "I take it they think you're out riding?"

She didn't look back at me. "They think I'm out weeping." She took a deep breath and glanced at me. "A Kiliok tradition before a wedding."

"Kiliok." I rolled that word around in my mouth. "A northern queen, very well."

She didn't so much nod as keep staring. "Do you know of us?"

I shrugged loosely, destabilizing clumps of dirt that

rolled down my shoulder-tops. "I know of many things."

A faint smile ghosted over her lips again. "Cool."

I shook my head and returned to examining the warm waters. "You know, perhaps you are safe from me eating you, but there are other, scarier things in this forest." I hit her with a hard look. "It's old. And the earth here is not as kind as me."

She looked nonplussed. "Scarier than you?" She grinned boldly. "I highly doubt it."

I huffed. "Perhaps you should act like it," I groused plainly, "and leave. That's what you do when you're scared, if you'd like to know."

"So touchy!" Tuck crowed. "It almost sounds like you like to be alone," she said cheekily, and I searched the waters for the nearest large fish.

"How did you guess?" I retorted in a flat tone, and she laughed.

"Go on," she said cheerily. "Catch something."

My lips curled back again. "You're already here."

"Oh, come now, we already had this out." She gathered her legs to her chest, reminding me of a small child or a cat. "I want to be you and you want to eat me. Neither of us can have what we want."

I gave her one last placid look before plunging my hand into the water; my long nails pierced the fish before it could even twitch. It was large, the largest one I had had in months, and I smiled greedily.

I wrenched the catfish from the waters and held its flopping body in my hands. "Watch carefully, young queen." My eyes gleamed. "You may learn something."

I sank my teeth into its moist flesh and waited for it to stop squirming before tearing at its soft meat.

"Cool," was the last word I heard before I dug in. I would have rolled my eyes all over again if I wasn't preoccupied.

Tuck was still there when I finished and asked me how I found rocs. Were they slightly above dog intelligence, or was it true you could hold a conversation with one? I tried to fade back into the muddy waters, but we ended up bickering about enchanted animals and where to best summon storms from.

∞∞∞

"I don't suppose you ever leave this place."

I came to expect Tuck's weekly visits, a two full moons' worth so far. I didn't turn around this time as she approached.

"Not like you do, Princess," I said somberly as I oozed my way toward the midday sun; she always came around midday.

"Ha, right," she said lightly and took her usual seat by my waters. "You could go wherever you please, though."

I raised my eyebrows and a stick dislodged from my hair and bumped my cheek before making a small *plop* into the water. I traced patterns in the algae in front of me. "And where would I go?"

Tuck made a soft sound. "I dunno. Another swamp? The coasts? The arctic wilds? You must have hobbies."

I fixed her with an even look. "Between you and the errant fisherman, I'm afraid I have no time for hobbies," I said gingerly and she let out her little snorting laugh.

"I'm serious."

I tsked. "I'm as bound to this swamp as you are bound to the land instead of sky. It is how it is," I said slowly.

She nodded a little sardonically. "Finally, straight answers."

I sighed. "Have you come to quiz me again about dwarven bathing habits?"

She smiled brightly. "That and, unfortunately, it seems Jace will have me do all the work for him."

"The Hessians usually do." I peered down at my long nails. "What is it?"

Her large green eyes held me for a second. "Are you free next Friday?"

I chuckled lowly. "Let me check my schedule."

Tuck returned the wicked smile. "I was told it was best to invite the local powerful Mythics." She winked. "Wouldn't want to snub anyone."

"After all the other visits? I wouldn't mind being snubbed at this point," I grumbled.

"Come now," she said heartily. "Scare a few nobles, get a free meal, remind the world that's it's mortal and weak and easily eaten by strange green ladies. You must like being invited to these sorts of things for a reason."

"It's a matter of honor," I said tightly, "respect."

She examined me again. "I see."

"No, you don't," I snapped back, and she laughed once more.

"Always so prickly!" she tutted. "You're lucky I like you, or I wouldn't invite you to my wedding."

"You just like oddities," I said in a dismissive tone. "Bored nobles like yourself so easily lose their common sense." I eyed her. "But I'll come. I do like to see the children's faces when I arrive," I finished with a sharp grin.

"That's the spirit." She beamed. "Now"—she settled down —"do you think the gods of night are better lovers than those of the sun? I've heard rumors going both ways."

"Of course, the moon ones are better," I said as I settled down deep into the silt of the pond bed with only my head exposed. "The sun gods are more self-centered than a nymph discovering her own reflection..."

I wished so desperately for Tuck to leave, but I never was good at giving in to myself either.

∞∞∞

The day came, a breezy morning in spring when the sun erupted out from between the clouds and flowers were set to bloom. There were very few flowers by my bridge, but I sensed them opening elsewhere. Their scent thick in the air, they rejoiced in the soil, covered in red ladybugs and fat yellow bees that feared the dark of my woods.

I dragged myself up and feasted, spending two days gorging and fueling myself for the journey. I cast golden protective circles around my limbs and throat. I caked more mud into my hair and fashioned branches into crooked wings off my hunched shoulders.

A bog hag had to play her part, after all; I had to show them what eternity looked like.

The actual exit from my realm was long and unnerving; the familiar suck of my life-force and the shuddering of every nerve in my body was taxing. I hefted myself slowly out of the water, groaning slightly like an oak tree against a typhoon.

The last push was always the hardest.

Solid ground was a cold kick to the teeth, and I was glad no one wandered near the edges of my bog as I finished the exodus. I took several deep, wincing breaths and straightened myself out.

"All right," I said calmly, "yes."

I summoned my strength back to me. The color returned to my cheeks and my hands steadied; it would be easy after that.

I did not walk the city streets, as that would in many ways ruin the effect. Instead, I arrived at the palace gates as a shadow and summoned the northern winds to blow open the doors. The first set of courtiers jumped at the banging of the wood and whoosh of the breeze. I spread my arms out wide and raised myself up tall. "Good morning."

I took in the children's faces first. Oh yes—their little bewildered stares were the cream for the cat's tongue. Their mouths were agape and their eyes as wide as moons. I could only grin at the hisses and hushed whispers of the adults as they witnessed me. I strode forward and watched their chests seize up and noses turn toward the ceiling. I walked on.

The floors were covered in blood-red carpet sheathed in gold trim, and silken tapestries hung on the walls of past wars and dead heroes. I didn't bother to soften my steps or hold my dirt clumps to me. I let the soil roll to the castle floors and earth-worms wiggle in my wake as they fell.

I made a beeline for the throne room and found a tall gray-ing man with steel eyes and a square jaw outside of it, waiting. He wore a white military uniform with a purple cape draped across his shoulders, and a golden crown glinted on his brow. I lifted my chin up.

"Kind as ever to invite me, King Gregory," I said huskily as I reached the enormous doors. I didn't have to look up to know I had the king's attention.

Every muscle in his body tightened. "It is an honor to host you, Miss Lamn." Lamn was the name of the bog I inhabited. They didn't know my real name, but that was how it was sup-posed to be.

I lifted my sharp chin up. "A witch always remembers loyalties, Sire. We both give and take." I emphasized the "give *and* take," reminding him of the long agreement between us: the diplomacy of the sword and bread. They offered me the bread, so I wouldn't brandish my sword. I nodded at their wisdom and exchanged a tablet of blood with the king—I would never harm his bloodline as long as he honored me.

"If you'll excuse me, Miss Lamn." He left as soon as the trade was over, and I turned back to the great hall. The crowd parted for me with enough room for a parade of horses between us. I grinned. *Oh yes, this part I like.*

I showed a nearby girl all five of my bare, busted teeth, and she made a small whimpering sound before hiding in her mother's skirts. I cackled and turn back to the main room, where the king was whispering to an advisor but making no move to approach me again. A smart man.

The queen of the fairies arrived shortly after and was greeted in a similar fashion. Hessia was a large kingdom and had quite a few powerful Mythics who could attend if they wanted to, but only a few would. Even I would admit that in other cases, I might have foregone the trip, but I was still a little perplexed by the future queen. I had been meeting her weekly, after all.

The locals watched me closely as I passed easily through the church doors with not so much as a twitch. *Like the devil works that simply, little fools.*

They scattered once I entered and looked in their direction.

I was unsurprised to read a different name on the parchment hanging inside the church. I shook my head at the welcoming sign: "The Wedding of Prince Jace to his betrothed Princess Nadina." I didn't know what to make of "Nadina," but perhaps everyone comes up with names for ourselves that are wildly different than ones we are given. Perhaps.

I climbed a set of designated stairs, took a seat on a closed-off balcony, and waited.

The scene reminded me of every other human wedding I had attended: stiff, formal, with uncomfortable shoes and frivolous hats. There was a small boy up front who kept unlacing his smock and throwing it off only to have mother tie it up all over again. I almost wanted to give him a smile, a real one that wouldn't haunt his dreams for life. But it was a fleeting thought.

The slow, respectable music began from the band, and I almost regretted attending. Queen Jinn arrived shortly and took a seat to my left and said nothing as the crowd settled down for the main event.

The fairy queen looked similarly bored and held her mouth in a taut, indifferent line. She was a tall creature with wavy purple hair, yellow cat eyes, and dark skin that glowed iridescently. A bracken crown sat on her head, and two enormous moth wings sprouted from her back. She watched sullenly as the performance conducted itself onward.

Prince Jace arrived with his back straight and his mouth an even straighter line. He looked like every other young man in his family line, and I didn't bother to memorize his face. He had licorice-black locks and cool blue eyes, an upright frame and a straight nose. I didn't see anything like Tuck in his bearing, but I wasn't sure what I expected.

Jace took his place next to the minister and looked toward the end of the grand space.

The music erupted in a melodic silver jingle and I paused, stilling myself for the next familiar clumsy footsteps. She was wearing heels this time, white and pristine and high as the heavens. Her gown trailed several people behind her, and she had flowers braided into her shimmering blond hair. Her dress was white, and the jewels around her throat were blood red—they seemed to wear her more than she wore them.

"They plucked that one from the edge of the Thirteen Kingdoms," Jinn murmured, and we exchanged a glance. "The kingdom of Kiliok is not known for strength." Jinn smiled with all her teeth. "And the prince would bargain for beauty over the brawn of a nation, it seems."

I frowned slightly. Of course Jace's family would choose someone from a place like Kiliok. The country wouldn't be able to request much from them or use their queen as a bargaining tool. Kiliok was too distant and small—it would have very little voice at court.

Tuck walked steadily down the aisle, and I examined the pearls embroidered into the bodice of her dress and the curve of the corset keeping her perfectly upright. She set a steady pace down the soft white aisle, and I forgot to hold my expression firmly blank. She reached the altar just as the minister began his monologue outlining duty and country, heirs and gold.

"Are you going to curse them?" Jinn asked mildly as we watched on.

I shook my head. "They've paid their dues," I said without blinking. "I have nothing to gain from it." I looked at her. "You?"

Her spotted wings fluttered behind her. "I considered a blessing."

I glanced at her. "Oh?"

She glanced down. "Or a curse. I still haven't decided. I'll have to see my mood."

I gave a rumbling chuckle and turned away. "Do as you will."

". . . and do you, Nadina Josephine Tulip . . ." I wondered

which name truly belonged to her as the procession wound down to the actual kiss. It didn't really matter, of course; their lips met in the end and the crowd erupted into applause.

A new queen was welcomed into the family—however foreign she might be.

Tuck only paused once to look up and give me a very curious look as she passed, arm in arm with Prince Jace. I gave her a short nod and she smiled. I let it all pass and considered leaving then.

"Oh." I looked up as Jinn spoke mildly.

I blinked. "Yes?" I prompted her and watched her finely crafted features shift; her lips pulled down and her pupils expanded. "Did you make up your mind?" I finally asked as she sat motionlessly beside me.

Jinn flashed a look at me and then turned her face away. "Humans make their own curses," she responded lowly.

My mouth twitched. "Ruins our business, doesn't it?"

She didn't laugh, and I didn't try to force it. Jinn smiled an alien smile and then left. The wedding of Nadina of Kiliok and Jace of Hessia passed without note for that night.

I watched the first dance and ate my fill of chicken and all the little lambs in the kingdom; I only stopped to tell one tale to the locals. It was a folk story of blood-eating giants and the ghosts of lost maidens in my bog. The maidens in white turned out to be banshees at the end, of course, and the look in the locals' eyes when I got to that part always made it worth it.

Tuck didn't spare me another glance.

I returned, exhausted, to my bog and waited for the next week. It came, and she did not. I waited for the next one, but no horse hooves or little clumsy feet approached from outside.

I tried to let go of the strange Tuck girl and her brief fascination with oddities.

She was just another bored noble, after all.

The sun set and rose, and the days passed on. Days and days, and then winters that I stopped counting.

∞∞∞

I was older by then, still around four hundred, young for the ages and old for myself.

Her footsteps returned on the night of the rains, heavy this time and with a purpose to them. The vibrations across the wood were lumbering, the lightness of her step was replaced with a thumping sturdy gait. I lifted my eyebrows. It was different, but it was still her.

The water washed against the top of my bridge, and I curiously stuck my head out; raindrops pelted across my nose as someone stood directly above me. She hadn't bothered to stay in the neutral zone this time.

She bent over the railing, drooping like her limbs might fall apart at the seams at any moment, heavy, and fit together with bolts and screws instead of feathers. I looked up and thunder crashed in the distance.

I frowned. "This isn't really the time or place, little bird."

I tried to make her out and noticed the shape of her dress had changed—no, her body had changed. I tried to remember how many years it had been, but out of the dark night, I made out a distinct slope of her dress, outward, a belly extending down.

I drew myself up. "There is a storm. You should know—"

"Help me."

Her face was illuminated by a lightning strike, and her features came into sharp focus: swollen cheeks and hollow eyes, complexion pale as a blurry full moon. Her hair clung damply to her face, and some life had been drained out of her.

I should turn her away quickly, threaten her back into the cas-

tle. I ordered myself to dismiss her.

"Please," she said in a tiny voice threaded with pure exhaustion.

I pointed to the nearest bog tree instead. "Curl up there," I murmured. "Close your eyes."

I cast the protection spell around the tree before I even knew what I was doing. *I shouldn't,* I told myself, *I don't want to.* But the spot was soon dry and plush as the water veered away from it and a young woman curled up underneath the branches.

The hours slipped by as I watched Tuck fall into a deep, troubled sleep under my watch. I didn't let the rain touch her.

Many hours faded through until the morning sun eventually punctured the misty cloud cover and I turned back to the woman. Her eyes slowly opened as the light pierced through the tree branches and I stared discerningly down at her midriff.

"You're with child," I said dryly as I licked my lips. "The heir." I gestured downward and tried to put together my next question.

Tuck's eyes flickered back and forth in a type of panic and she slowly sat up. "It wasn't a dream." She clutched her loose shawl around herself.

"Shhh." I hovered closer. "You've simply had a bad night, little bird."

She glanced over at me and her eyes were as sunken as craters on the moon. "You," she said breathlessly, "Lamn."

I nodded slowly. "Among other names."

I watched carefully as Tuck's eyes filled with moisture and started to overflow. She curled up on herself and cradled her swollen belly. "I thought I dreamed you too."

I shook my head. "Tuck," I said calmly, and she looked up immediately, responding to what must have been an old name by then. "You carry the heir. Someone must be looking for you by now."

And I don't fancy being swamped by an angry mob right now.

She shivered from head to toe and I observed her thin wrists and puffy face. Something was wrong. She looked up at me with her bottom lip trembling. "It doesn't matter," she said in a hiccupping voice. "Let them look."

I frowned deeply. "What is it?" I asked, dragging my eyes over her sickly pale skin. "What is all this?"

She looked down at her lap, eyes burning. "Lamn, this child feels as if it might kill me," she said faintly, with a bow to her head. "It feels like it *is* killing me."

I waited for a moment, assessing her withered look, drooping posture, and the steel in her eyes. I took a deep, unhappy breath. "It is never easy."

She shook her head and the tears kept overflowing. "I can't sleep. The nausea is constant. He keeps moving. He's . . . it's not going right. It's all wrong."

I pursed my lips. "I can see the sickness on you."

She let out a little sob. "Did you do this?" Her eyes crinkled. "I didn't think you cursed me, but . . ."

I shook my head. "I am not the person you think I am."

She looked down at her lap again and blinked a couple times. "I know," she said, and her voice cracked. "I told Jace it was me and not you. That I'm the reason for it." She hid her face in her hands, and I eased myself down next to her.

"Hush now." I patted her shoulder.

She painfully looked up with puffy red eyes. "Please," she said in a voice I never heard her use before, "can you help me?"

I nodded. I didn't want to. I knew I shouldn't. But it was too late—it had been too late for a while.

"Reed root," I said simply. "Mandrake placed in warm milk," I continued. "Honey mixed with temple rot—not the mold kind, the roots."

She wrinkled her brow. "The doctors have been working around the clock. Do you think . . . ? Do you know . . . ?" She grasped at something and searched my face.

JACQUELYNN LYON

I slowly raised my thin, gnarled hands up toward her. "And one last thing."

She blinked a couple times. "Yes?"

"My blessing." I whispered and sucked the light dry from the air around me. "Don't tell anyone."

The light hovered, brave and new, twinkling in the air around us like stars. I hadn't given one out in ages—not since I was fresh, and young. The light scattered in all directions and then sucked into her skin and pores as I said the words under my breath, welding them to her.

"Light, protection, breath," I murmured. "Light, protection, breath." I weaved her lifeline together so thick and golden that I thought she might live forever after that. I took a deep breath and opened my eyes that I hadn't realized I'd closed. "That child is not going to kill you, Your Majesty."

Tuck was still weeping. She was older somehow, so much older. "Thank you," she said breathlessly. "Gods, thank you."

I took her hand and repeated, "Mandrake soaked in warm milk, honey mixed with temple rot—just the roots." We shared a look that I couldn't describe, and I wanted to shatter that, too, gnash it up between my teeth and forget.

Her shoulders were thick and heavy looking, sloping down and finally releasing. "They wouldn't let me see you after we started trying for him. They said I had to stay inside the castle for the sake of my health." She held her belly again, and I nodded.

"It's for the best," I responded tartly and looked away.

She sighed with the weight of ages on her. "I don't suppose bog hags have to give their lives for duty and country?"

I gave a sad smile. "Go back, little bird," I said and closed my eyes. "The grass is not greener in pastures you know not of."

She raised her eyebrows. "I always read that bog witches were full of riddles. You've been holding out on me."

I gave a soft chuckle, and the old Tuck I remembered shone through this new, mature woman.

I reached, and I knew I shouldn't either, but it was too

80

late now. I took both her soft, milky hands and I squeezed them, hard, not hard enough to hurt. But she needed to know.

"This child will not kill you," I whispered with a hiss. "You have my blessing. Use it."

She looked down toward her belly reverently. "Will he have it too?"

I frowned. "You shouldn't tell anyone."

She cooed softly. "You hear that little one?" She gave a smile that glowed at the edges. "You will be imbued with essence of bog witch."

I snorted. "You always were more daring than a box of feral cats."

She looked up, sadly this time. "Thank you," she said, face still swollen and eyes sunken. "I won't forget this."

I started to shoo her. "Go," I said quickly, something stirring within me, "before I change my mind."

She rolled her eyes but managed to lumber to her feet. "This won't be the last you see of me, Lamn," she said softly and began to walk. "Not this time." I watched her back as she retreated toward the bridge and toward her people.

My eyes creased and I exhaled. "It's Clemency," I called listlessly after her. "Lamn is the name of the bog."

She was gone already, and I had nothing but a sudden pain left in my chest. I closed my eyes and extended the blessing once more.

∞∞∞

Tuck returned twice. Once to tell me that the mandrake screamed at her and to curse me for it, and another time to laugh so hard she almost fell into the swampy waters next to me. Jace apparently almost passed out when he saw her eating temple rot.

She got better.

I heard from afar that the next prince was born, just as the old King Gregory died. Tuck really was a queen now. It was a closed birth, a hard pregnancy and a hard birth. No one was invited to it.

I felt her distant footsteps now and then. Sometimes they came to the edge of the bog, but they never entered. I waited. I didn't dwell. I slept soundly as several winters passed in a blur.

I left once, into the city streets, disguised as a beggar woman, and I heard that the new prince was strong, rambunctious. He had his father's charcoal-black hair and his mother's smile. I tried not to catch his name, and I did anyway.

Clement.

I didn't dwell on it.

∞∞∞

was steeped in the roots of a tree when I heard it again—something I thought had disappeared from my stratosphere forever.

"I can't," she spoke rapidly, breathlessly. "I tried to. But I can't, not again."

I turned around slowly, easily. I straightened up and oozed down the roots and back toward my bridge. I raised my eyebrows. "And here I thought you were a smart girl and were done with me."

Tuck's lips quivered. She was dressed in an olive-green gown and looked bright and full of life this time. "Never," she said softly, and I didn't know what to do with that.

"Huh," I grunted and turned away again.

She took a deep breath. "I tried to take him to meet you," she said steadily as she looked down from her perch on the bridge, "again and again. But they watch him more carefully than a hawk watches a field mouse."

I sank into the muddy waters. "As they should."

She frowned deeply. "They don't trust me."

I nodded. "A foreign queen stays foreign for a land like

Hessia," I said grimly. "I know well of these people's superstitions."

She gave a tight smile down at the ground. "I started reading all those books you told me about," she said in a small voice. "They keep me sane."

"Did you ever figure out if fairies are actually clever or not?"

Tuck looked up. "I did," she said slowly. "They are. But not as clever as they think."

I gave a hearty laugh, a real one. "Smart girl."

Tuck tightened her hands around each other. "No." She looked away. "I was foolish."

I shrugged. "You were young," I said as I tilted my head. "Different, strange, and not sorry about it."

She grinned thinly. "Still am." She sighed. "But I made so many mistakes." She rubbed her knuckles together. "I never earned their trust."

I tilted my head to the side. "Why are you telling me this?" My jaw tightened.

"I don't know." She sighed heavily. "Perhaps I wanted one last confession, or maybe I thought it might change something. To go where it all began."

"What began?"

She looked up at the tree branches above. "It doesn't matter," she said bitterly and closed her eyes. "They want me to do it again."

I raised my eyebrows. "Do what?" I said flatly. "Wander into bogs again and bother ancient, powerful beings?"

She laughed. "I wish!" She took a deep, heaving breath. "They need more than just Clement. Hessia demands multiple heirs."

"Oh." I nodded at that, affirming the truth I already knew. "Don't they know?" *Don't they know the first one was a hair away from killing you?*

She frowned at her feet. "They don't listen."

I nodded again. "I can . . ." I hummed. "I can do it again." I should have added "for a price," but I didn't.

She tugged at a stray blond lock of hair. "I don't have it in me. Not a second time," she said, looking weary, eyes tired and hands falling still and open at her sides, "even with a powerful witch's blessing."

I put my hand out. "You don't know what I'm capable of." I flashed her an almost-smile. "You never did."

She hesitated, looking at my hand for a long second, and I should have pulled back, but I didn't. She took it. Our skin met and tingled like a wildfire, and it wasn't like the first time, like when I was trying to convey everything to her.

She held the dust and the grime and my long-gnarled fingers; she brought them up toward her face. "I've been reading," she said evenly, eyes unfocused. "Tell me then," she whispered into my knuckle, "how does a river nymph descend into a bog?"

I didn't meet her eyes, but I tightened my grip. "With a bit of luck," I said warmly, and she chuckled.

"Of course." She searched my face with her prickly green eyes. "What kind of luck?"

I hummed deep in my chest. "It goes like all stories go. Life gives and takes. Power and hunger mixed in men who wanted with a want that carves out your flesh and digs out spirit and soul. Then I was given a blessing." I curled back my lips. "You already knew that secret, though."

She nodded and her free hand raised up and grazed my cracked cheek. "I wanted it so badly." Her eyes shimmered and met mine, holding my gaze and passing something unnamable between us; I leaned forward but didn't press any closer.

We held our breaths and waited for something that wasn't coming, wrapped in something we didn't understand. I clutched her hand so tightly I knew it hurt.

Tuck turned before I did, and we said a soundless goodbye. I threw my blessing at her one last time.

∞∞∞

Men . . . men are cruel. They fight and scream and ruin each other, arguing and crying to gods, falling in love and then out, hurting, only to do it all over again. Men are cruel. So are the waves and the stinging snow and biting wind and unforgiving earth. The earth is also cruel.

Though men can be bargained with, reasoned with, the earth, on the other hand, will eat you whole without question. Perhaps that was what I liked about it.

Her footsteps came heavy this time, fast and pounding the water's bottom, shoes sucked into the mud and struggling with each step. She was breathing hard and dashing forward with lurching, hurried movements.

I woke with a start as dogs brayed in the distance. She hadn't been subtle, or perhaps the king had more eyes on her side than she knew. Either way, I could feel the thumping of men's feet in my realm and the calling of distant voices.

I surged upright and moved as fast as a roaring river.

"Tuck!" I called with the voice of thunder. "Tuck!"

I could sense someone else cradled in her arms and squirming. "Mama." I heard it now, clear as day. He was young and strong, as I knew he would be.

I used the trees as my eyes and looked toward the scene. I found them.

The eyes of the boy glowed yellow in the dark and Tuck sprinted across the swampy earth, away from the dogs and the harsh voices. I surged forward on a wave of water, approaching quickly just as the soldiers did. The mother and child were pinned between me and the king's men.

I gnashed my teeth as I locked eyes with the distant footmen. "I will grind your bones to dust and use your shins as my garden gate," I roared and the men faltered, but only for a moment.

"A witch!"

"I knew it! I knew the unnatural queen had allies on the Other Side."

I flared my nostrils and I lifted my hand, but so did the

men. One young soldier raised a crossbow toward my chest and took aim right past Tuck's shoulder.

"Don't hit the child!" the captain cried as the young soldier was jostled from the side, and it all happened in slow motion.

"Clemency!" Tuck's voice rang out just as she reached for me, just as the arrow was let loose.

Her son's eyes went huge, his body shaking as the arrow pierced his mother's back like a sapling pierces the soft earth as it grows. A silent gasp spread across Tuck's face and then a shock of pain. Clement fell from her arms and she toppled forward. Red blossomed across the dark waters.

I gave out an unearthly cry, every inch of me tingling as I prepared to descend on the soldiers. I would make sure they were dead and eaten and discarded into the scraps of time and earth. I screamed and screamed, but I was not the only one listening.

Before my winds could wrench apart the woods, before the roaches could come crawling out of the trees and bog cats yowling out of the ground, before I could summon hell—the earth was listening, and the earth does not bargain, but it does give and take.

Much like a witch.

It encompassed her before I could even blink, the vines and leaves and waters swishing around her, covering her, folding around her from all sides.

I needed to rip out the throats of these men, but I picked up her wailing son instead. He was weeping and wiping at his brilliant yellow eyes and tearing at his dark hair, whimpering softly in an emotion I couldn't fathom from one so young.

"Shhh." I gathered him close to me. "It's beginning."

The leaves twisted, the waters rippled, and the forest became so deathly quiet I was afraid it might break. They call it the devil, but I have never seen the devil breathe life back into someone as quickly as he takes it.

Her skin fastened into thick bark, her hair twisted into

streams of golden light, her face mixed into something other-worldly and unknowable, rough and hard in all directions. Tuck rose once more from the waters, and I was left breathless. She stood, bark and light and forest now, all forest.

She raised her head and smiled, smiled something brilliant and wicked. "I knew it," she said softly and looked down at her hands.

The soldiers scattered, running for their lives to tell the king of the betrayal; terror would follow horror. But that could wait. It all could wait. I shifted young Prince Clement in my arms and reached out one last time.

She took my hand. "Tell me," she said lightly, "can a bog witch fall in love? I read that they can't."

I smiled widely. "Let's find out."

We turned toward the deepest parts of the forest and started walking, creeping into the unknown depths of a soft and distant world. The first kiss shifted everything inside me, and the second one broke it.

Very few new footsteps arrived after that, for who would face the two most powerful bog witches in their home? Two witches and the next and future king.

We Deserve a
Soft Landing, Love

Year: 2036

Astronauts really weren't supposed to be alone. Not at the space station. It wasn't made to run that way. Three permanent residents were assigned at all times, and they were rarely alone.

But mistakes happen. A gash the size of her forearm ran down his side, perfectly round, and red droplets hung in the air like ping-pong balls in suspended animation. A face as ashen as the grave and yelling. They never yelled.

Sarah Reyes was chosen for her composed personality—composed in theory, less so in practice. She watched her co-worker burst open and heard NASA ringing in her ear: *What do you even do with a dead body in space?*

But he wasn't gone yet.

They pressed a template they never had before: срочный спуск. The Soyuz computer sprang to life: *Emergency Landing.*

NASA kept ringing in her ears. Some young woman named Janet was talking to her now, and she was talking back.

Rod wasn't going to make the journey if he went back alone. His eyes were barely open, and red, blooming droplets still swam around the room like liquid party balloons. Sarah never liked the word "helpless."

She looked to Nikolai and told him to "get the fuck down there"; someone needed to take the CRV shuttle down with him. Nikolai's heavy-lidded eyes studied her, he pursed his lips, and she said it once more in Russian and then again in English.

They secured Rod's bandage a second time, his fever-warm face a distant star on the horizon. She grabbed onto his hand and told them to "get the fuck down there."

They pressed срочный спуск. The shuttle launched down with Kazakhstan readying down below. God, they had to be ready.

And she was alone.

Astronauts were not supposed to be alone.

The quiet was just as engulfing as the urgency had been before. Janet had apparently gone to take a break, and they were on the sun side of the planet. Sarah started counting. It would take them three-and-a-half minutes to get back to Earth. It would take three days for a shuttle to come back to the station. It would take three hours for the shuttle to be attached to the docking port.

It would take some undisclosed amount of time for them to sort out the politics down below. Astronauts don't just burst open. And Sarah was alone.

She continued as normal. There was nothing else to do. She had—at the very least—three days to herself, and there was cleaning to do. Maintenance, communication. It turned into four days.

She was talking to a young man named Ted on the telecom now, and she was sort of starting to hate young men named Ted. Politics were messier than space, and no one was even set up to relieve her yet. NASA was in some sort of limbo, and Russia wasn't talking. Sarah was alone.

It was the sixth day when the shuttle finally launched, a crew of three. Sarah had already forgotten their names, but she would have months to memorize them anyway.

She had turned off the intercom for that day, and she didn't notice the static until later when it started echoing in the hallways like a ghost. Sarah didn't believe in ghosts, though. No self-respecting scientist believed in ghosts.

They were on the planet side of the sun, dark, alone, dumping heat back into the square hallways through the vents.

Sarah heard the first hush of static in her sleep, strapped down and frowning deeply as she screwed her eyes shut. It felt like she was getting tinnitus. For a moment, she refused to wake up—she had to keep to her schedule, or else what the fuck else was she going to have up there?

The static breathed again, and her thoughts broke off and on in starts. Finally, she sat up. After all, they don't know what to do with dead bodies in space. She ripped her sleeping mask off and cocked her head to the side.

Ssshhhhhh

She squirmed out of her restraints and floated to the side of the room. "It's probably just Yulia messing with the frequencies planet-side," she muttered to herself, mostly just to hear the sound her own raw voice in the dark. "Just Yulia . . ."

She pulled herself up and out and floated over to the communication bay while passing the wide, yawning emptiness of the station. It could technically suit ten people, the size of a five-person house, but apparently, Earth was still arguing. Two more days.

Sssshhhhhhh

She sighed and followed the noise; she really wasn't in the mood for any system malfunctions. She tapped on the screen of the newly installed HD video chat. It sprang to life with the headquarters of NASA asking who she would like to get a hold of today.

Sarah blinked. No one had been hailing her.

Sssshhhhhh

She looked around, and the hairs on the back of her neck stood on end. None of the devices in the room were lighting up or winking at her. None of them were making any sounds at all. She scratched the back of her hand and accepted the fact that the noise really wasn't coming from the central communication room.

Sarah turned around in meaningless circles, and then left a message to the NASA night crew that there was a possible technical issue on the ISS. Two days before any crew was set to land, Sarah groaned, and it was just her.

She took deep breaths and pushed herself off toward what she could only assume was the source of the noise.

Ssssshhhh

She cringed as she crossed the "unity" room to the Russian side of the station, empty as a ghost town and twice as unnerving. But Sarah didn't believe in ghosts.

Ssssshh-he-sssshh–ll-ssh-o

"Ah!" She clutched at her heart as something, a voice something, echoed off the walls. She took a deep, rasping breath and turned in every direction.

Ssh, hello? It came again.

Sarah's mouth hung open, and she found herself outside of a room that had been used as an old communication hub. It was a relic from a time back when they had separate ones instead of a "bubble of trust" in the center of the station.

Sarah cocked her head to the side and stared. One of the old radios that was attached to the wall and ingrained in the system was making a soft, but distinct, buzz. It was gray and had a panel of buttons and a microphone attached to a round speaker. Most of the old, pre–2025 devices had been removed or repurposed, but this one was intact. It felt like she was reaching backward in time itself.

She frowned at it, and she knew she should go report this. Houston would want to know one of the 2000 models was acting up.

Shhh-h–ssss

Sarah reached forward, her finger hovered in midair over the panel, and her eyes became glued to the intercom. There was something, a voice something, bubbling underneath the static.

And, of course, she *did* believe in aliens.

Sarah pressed down on a feedback button and wet her lips. Then she leaned down toward the speaker. "Is someone there?"

She held her breath and watched the blinking red light of the transmitter in the dark center of the room. It had been re-purposed several years ago to be another storage room.

She blinked, waited a full minute, and suddenly felt a lit-tle silly—she should really be sleeping right now. Or reporting it. She watched the flickering red light and counted.

It was 60 seconds, 180 seconds, 3 minutes. Sarah was about to take her finger off the feedback button when some-thing responded back with clear articulation.

"Oh, thank God."

Sarah's mouth fell open. It was a woman. She quickly bent over to reply, but the voice kept going.

"Can you hear me? Is someone there? I am Lotte De Vos of the Argus, Landing Mission One, ESA. Can you hear me?"

Sarah gasped. "Oh my God—"

Lotte kept speaking quickly, "We have been pushed out off route and . . . Can anyone hear me?"

"Yes!" Sarah returned as soon as she found her voice again, perhaps yelling into the speaker a little too loudly. "We thought —I—are you safe? We thought the Argus was lost. What's your status?"

Sarah did the math in her head; it would take four to five minutes for radio waves to transmit between Earth's orbit and the Argus: the Jupiter moon's mission.

"I can't see our location, but I think I am stranded near the atmosphere of Jupiter. Repeat, I can see the troposphere. . . . I don't know where I am."

"Argus," Sarah rushed to speak, hoping they could balance out their conversation amid the delays, "I am Sarah Reyes of the International Space Station, NASA. I can hear you loud and clear. What's your status?"

She waited. Counting sixty seconds, two minutes, three minutes, God, she needed to tell someone about this. But then she heard the sharp intake of breath on the other end.

"ISS?" the woman responded. "Thank God. Okay, this is Lotte De Vos, reporting again from the Argus. The . . . the life support system is sustaining itself, it looks like. But none of the rams are responding. I think we're disconnected from the rockets."

"Miss De Vos," Sarah said as she hunched over, "what is the status of the crew? How much oxygen do you have left? What . . . what happened?" She remembered reading about the Argus a week ago: about the radio silence on the other end of one of the most ambitious human-manned missions into their solar system.

One minute. Two minutes. Three. Four.

"I . . . I have the full amount of oxygen left that we carried with us for the return journey." She paused, and a hitch of static filled the air. "The crew is incapacitated," her voice said flatly. "We were hit with an unexpected projectile and were pulled into Jupiter's orbit. We didn't calculate the full effect of the planet's mass on our ship, it seems." She chuckled, and it was one of the most surprising sounds Sarah had ever heard. "I guess we are still making scientific discoveries."

"Do you have your satellite? Where is your telecom? We can—"

The delay continued to confuse their conversation. "—it's acting like a black hole. We tried to fix the rockets to propel us back to the base on Io, but there wasn't enough power. Everyone else . . ." The woman took a deep, shaking breath. "They tried to get back to it without the ship. Some of our jets were still working for the suits."

"Oh my God," Sarah whispered.

"It didn't work."

Sarah waited, making sure Lotte was finished and the full four to five minutes had passed so Lotte could get Sarah's message.

She heard another laugh on the other side. "We really need a better system than this. How about we say 'over' when we're done talking?"

Sarah's shoulders tensed. The woman sounded so young.

"Anyway, to answer your question, our telecom was damaged when the projectile thrust us off course. I just recently jury-rigged this device in order to be picked up on low frequencies." Lotte took an audible breath. "Over."

Sarah pressed her forehead up against the cool metal of the side paneling; she cleared her throat. "Lotte," she said quietly, "do you need me to contact anyone?" It had taken that crew six years to get to Jupiter's moons. "Over."

Sarah squeezed her eyes shut. She heard the next notes like a deflating balloon.

"So, you've figured it out too?" Lotte said with a controlled tremor to her voice. "Well . . . I have a few people I would like to message if you could write it down. Over."

Sarah floated to the side of the makeshift storage room and found a pen and paper. She wrote down the woman's mother's name, her college professor's email, and her ex-lover's phone number.

"Do you want me to"—Sarah cringed—"uh, write down messages for them? For me to say to them? Over."

She waited, then she heard a sigh when the four minutes passed.

"Just tell my mom I love her. That sort of thing. Tell the professor I wouldn't be here without her, I mean, not here, in space, in a bad way, shit, actually, don't tell her that. Tell her that her intro classes are still making freshman wet themselves, and I love it."

Sarah laughed. "And the last one?" she asked as she waited for Lotte to come back to her.

Lotte gave a snort. "Flip her off for me. Maybe subtly infer she's been skipping arm day and is looking a little noodly. That would make my night. Over."

Sarah chuckled deeply, and it was hard for her to take it all in. She should be writing more down, she thought. She should be writing it all down. "You know," she began as thoughts ran through her head like a speeding, stop-and-go traffic jam, "are the rockets really not working? Because a simple continued jury-rig of the thrusters back to the navigation might, hmm, help."

The response took longer than usual. "Don't do this to me," came the hushed reply. "I've tried, Sarah. Don't you think I've tried? Whoever you are, from wherever, don't do it."

"Sarah Reyes," she repeated slowly, blinking into the dark. "I'm from Minneapolis."

Lotte hummed. "Oh . . . I'm from Belgium. Ghent. Nice to meet you."

Sarah's insides felt like they were turning all over the place. "I've been to Belgium. It's very beautiful."

"Not underwater yet?" the other woman joked, slightly offbeat due to the time lapse.

"They're trying their best," Sarah said with a sniff. "And they never invented a statute called 'The Twinkie Law,' so they did better than my city."

She heard a strange groan from the other end of the line, which made Sarah sit up straight. "I would honestly give anything right now for a Twinkie. Anything."

Sarah ended up laughing. "All right, top ten food goos and then worst goos, go."

Lotte made a choking sound. "Nooo, Sarah Reyes, all I want right now is some ripe cherries, a medium rare steak, fuck it, a rare steak, and ten Twinkies, one for every finger. No goo."

Sarah was snickering. "Well, I want a nice hamburger and maybe a salad with ranch dressing. Kleenexes. Running water." She smiled to herself. "And a proper toilet."

The silver sound of a laugh came back from the other end. "Wrong answer! The whole reason I went to space was for suction toilets."

"Oh no, no, no. Come. On," she said emphatically.

"What we all really need is at least one beer each," Lotte bemoaned. "A margarita, two lagers, some vodka—good vodka, the kind the Russians would give to their moms."

Sarah snorted and shook her head. "Why did you go to space then?" she asked fondly to the other end. "It's the last dry county in humanity's jurisdiction, Dutch girl."

Lotte huffed another laugh on the other end. "We're getting personal now? Well, you first. Why are you in space, hurtling above the Earth and developing poor bone mass?"

Sarah let herself float up a little higher and used the next minute to think about her answer. Then she leaned toward the speaker. "Height."

The five minutes passed, and all that came back was a confused "What?"

"I gain two and a half inches every time I come up here. Eventually, I figure I'll hit five feet."

A loud guffaw came back. "Taller! Of course, but what is that in human measurements?"

Sarah rolled her eyes. "Old habits. It's 6.35 centimeters and 1.5 meters, happy?"

"Woof," Lotte barked back cheerily. "They really do bring them in smaller each year. Over."

Sarah exhaled dramatically. "Back to you then, Miss Lotte. How tall are you? And, I don't know, what's your favorite, hmm, tea?"

Two minutes, three, four.

"Tea? Boring. Do you know how close Jupiter's atmosphere is to me right now? Ask me about my childhood nightmares and favorite sex position." Sarah opened her mouth to respond with a dismissive sniff, but Lotte added quietly at the end, "It's mint, by the way. Peppermint."

Sarah smiled, and she squeezed her eyes shut for a full minute. "Well, my childhood nightmare was Santa having literal claws and strangling me," Sarah said good-humoredly as she drummed her fingers on her leg and counted the seconds.

"Is that your favorite position, as well?"

"Lotte," she said with a warning tone and considered turning back around toward the communication hub. The next five minutes left her contemplating if it was a crank call—Houston did have some annoying interns.

"Strangling is perfectly natural—no need to be ashamed. I did it to my Barbie Dolls and everything."

Sarah rolled her eyes. "They really do send them up crazier each year."

Lotte laughed, and it was a strained sound with a tin undertone. Sarah pursed her lips together.

"Sarah?" Lotte said, barely audible over the static this time.

"Yeah?" She waited.

"Can you see Earth?"

Sarah hunched over, and she nodded meaninglessly before taking her finger off the feedback button and floating back over to the observatory. Two hours had passed since they started talking.

She looked out over a deep-brown storm cloud above China, a few glowing tendrils of cities and roads, and the textured darkness of the Earth side of the sun. She went back to the transmitter. "We're over the Bahamas. It's blue right now. Very, very blue."

She heard the softest of sounds over the radio. "My hull is made of titanium," Lotte said carefully, "but I'm not sure if the radio waves will be disturbed by the planet's magnetic field."

"Oh," Sarah said back, squeezing her eyes shut, knowing Lotte was still talking.

"And then the radiation will begin anyway." Lotte made something that was almost a laugh. "Remember those numbers, okay? Tell my mom. You know. Tell my teacher I wasn't going to make it without her, but not in this way. And tell Anika to, you know, fuck off."

"Wait," Sarah said breathlessly.

"I'm about to be sucked into the atmosphere. Wait a little for me, 'kay? We can see if this mess of a radio might hold up. Just wait a little. Then go tell the world I went out fighting. Fighting aliens or a space octopus. Tell them that there are definitely space octopuses, and the Argus went down swinging."

"Okay," Sarah rasped, holding the button down until the tip of her finger bleached white. "Okay!" She racked her brain for what to say, what eulogies people ended with or final, lasting sentiments that maybe meant something. "I'll eat some Twinkies for you. Ten. One for each finger."

Sarah waited. Two minutes. Three minutes. Five. Sarah was shaking. This isn't what she expected when she woke up that morning. The station orbited into the sun side of the planet. What was she even going to tell Houston? How do you start that report?

Sarah rubbed her stinging eyes. "I'll put them on my fingers too. Eat them in some Dutch coffee shop and kick your ex in the shins." She pushed her palms into her eye sockets. "Oh God. Oh my God."

Numbness ran up and down her legs, and she floated away from the feedback button. She was still glad she didn't believe in ghosts—she really didn't need this one.

She turned back to exit the room and float to somewhere far away and cold and curl up for a little bit.

Shhh—Hey! Loser!

Sarah jumped and turned around instantaneously. "Lotte?!" She jammed her finger on the transmission button.

"Can you hear me? I can't see out my window right now, but the magnetism might not be messing with my radio as much as I thought. More discoveries for science, yay. Have them name a cockroach after me or something. Unless, of course, you can't hear me and this is just, you know, the death chasm I'm speaking into—"

"I can hear you!" Sarah yelled as her finger cramped on the switch. The red light flared like a foghorn. "I can hear you! It's still working!" She didn't know why she was excited; this girl was entering into one of the most radioactive places in the solar system. Sarah kept her eyes on the speaker.

A tired exhale answered, "You waited after all."

Sarah bit her lip. "Yeah. I waited."

The four minutes were excruciating. "I figure I have

around forty-five minutes. . . . Anyway, if you're curious, it is incredibly hot. If I didn't have any decency left, I would be naked right now."

Sarah sniffed. "No one can see you, you know. And I imagine it's burning up."

The next transmission was garbled, but she could still make it out. "Dying in the void of space is one thing; dying in the void of space butt naked is another."

Sarah couldn't get herself to laugh this time, but she tried. "Well, I'll tell everyone you were wearing a full suit of armor. Pearls. Evening gloves. The octopus didn't stand a chance."

Lotte made a soft sound. "That's really all I ask. Heels too. I miss heels. I felt tall, like one of those small dogs on top of tables? Or the fact that you enjoy getting five centimeters taller in space?"

Sarah made an exasperated noise. "I don't suppose you mock all the people you share last words with?"

Lotte gave a soft chuckle. "Just you, darling." A long pause followed, and Sarah didn't move to fill it. Lotte took her time with another slow, hissing breath. "Tell me about something."

Sarah blinked. "I have a collection of coins from the Ottoman empire."

"Okay," Lotte sounded faint, "who was your first crush? Besides sixteenth-century sultans or something, I mean. What was your first book? What's your favorite kiss? Come on." Lotte snickered weakly. "I'm dying here."

Sarah's skin felt too tight, itching in the dark. "My first crush was Martina Rodriquez. Fifth grade, she punched me in the face once after I told her that her nose was crooked. I learned to read when I was three, so I don't really remember the books, accelerated learning and all that. I learned to speak in full sentences when I was six. My first kiss was . . ." Sarah sighed. "Don't laugh, okay? In my college's chemistry lab, age twenty-three." She said all of it quickly with pained breaths. Time was measured in fours and fives.

A laugh came back from the other side of the universe

anyway. "Chemistry lab? God, you're the one giving astronauts a nerdy name."

"Hey!"

"And it's cute. You sound cute. I'm sure you're very smart, too. You can probably name way too many numbers of pi." She could. "I guess I was like that too . . . Why I'm up here." Lotte trailed off.

"Why are you up here?" Seven minutes passed.

"I saw Cassiopeia one night. . . . My grandpa told me they hung her upside down in the night sky to punish her. I fell in love." Sarah clenched her jaw tight. "I guess you could say that's how it happened. Love or whatever."

"Lotte—" Sarah put her face next to the speaker.

"You know, I always thought this is what I wanted to do." Lotte was faltering. "And it is." She repeated with a slight hysteria and frantic edge to her words, "I think it was always what I wanted to do. Always."

There came a pause and Sarah heard a strangled retching noise on the other side.

"Lotte!" she yelled into the intercom. "Lotte, are you all right?"

It took a very long time before she got a response.

"Yeah," a voice finally said hoarsely. "Just . . . puking. You know, when you get to see food goo all over again? That feeling." Lotte sounded like she was trying to laugh. "Sarah?"

"Yeah?"

"Who was this first kiss?" Lotte asked quietly before sniffing. "Was she cuter than me? I hope not. . . . And then, what's —what's your favorite tea?"

Sarah squeezed her free hand closed, balling it up into a painful fist and digging her nails in. "No. She was a PhD student and thought that Potato Poots was a good pet name. She"— Sarah snorted—"wasn't cuter than you, promise. My favorite tea is black tea. I used to drink it with my aunts."

Two minutes. Three minutes. Six.

"Potato Poots? Take that back. That is a wonderful pet

name, and now I'm going to date this girl who was your first kiss." Sarah chuckled. "Black tea is a good choice. The closest one to coffee. My brother owns a coffee shop." Lotte was talking quickly now. "Visit him too. Tell him . . . I'm sorry. I'm sorry we fought so much, God, for everything."

"Yes, yes, I mean—"

"Tell all of them I loved them. Dammit, even Anika, tell her to get her shit together. None of this . . . none of anything else. Nothing else matters."

Sarah sighed, and her entire body was shaking. "I can do that, yes. Lotte, we won't forget."

"That I died naked in the void of space?" Lotte returned back after seven minutes. "Because that's a thing now."

"Naked, fighting an octopus, right?" Sarah said with her face straining into a smile.

"Yeah." Lotte was panting on the other end now, but her voice came through. "Who was your first love, Sarah?"

Sarah felt her mouth go dry. She hadn't drank anything in hours. Houston would be furious. "I've never been in love," she whispered back. "I just wanted to do . . . this." She flinched at the wording.

Lotte took eight minutes to respond. "Yeah?" she said breathlessly. "Well, do that for me, 'kay? Being in love is nice. It's like this, except no one is riding into the next layer of Jupiter's helium."

Sarah gave a weak smile. "It's like this?"

"It's like this," Lotte wheezed. "Go do that for me."

"How're you feeling?" Sarah tried to get her to keep talking, and Lotte told her that she threw up again. Sarah could hear strained breathing through the speaker. Lotte was gasping.

"We weren't really over the Bahamas, were we?"

Sarah frowned, and she looked toward where the window would be. "It was dark out, yeah. But the cities were bright. Like stars. We always liked stars, right? People like us?"

"People like us collect Ottoman coins and cover their hands in Twinkies, Sarah."

She smiled. "Good. I hear that's what being in love is like."

Lotte coughed, a deep, gurgling sound that filled the air. "Sounds dumb."

"It is."

Sarah could hear her fading out. "Lotte? Lotte how're you —"

"Fuck, fuck, fuck—" A sob shook the speaker.

"Lotte."

"FUCK, I don't want to die."

"Wait, wait, no, it's going to be okay."

"Quick, tell me something nice to say, something good. God, GOD, I wish I had been good. I wish had been better."

"Wait! Wait, no."

"Sarah."

She could hear the crying now, the sickly wet tremor in her voice.

"Sarah, I can't see anything. It's so hot. Oh my God, I can't do this, SARAH—"

Sarah screamed back into the mic, "I'm here! I'm here! Wait!"

No sound came back from the other side. Sarah's eyes went wide, and she counted up to a thousand. She couldn't feel her teeth.

One thousand and four, one thousand and five. "Lotte? Lotte De Vos, can you hear me?" Five minutes. Ten minutes.

Sarah curled up into herself and pulled on her hair, her other finger still on the transmission button and the room bathed in the one red light.

"Lotte," she blared. "Lotte!" It was a wretched, animalistic scream, but it wasn't for the radio; it wasn't for her.

She wished she believed in ghosts.

Sarah Reyes went back to Earth within the fortnight. She told them she wasn't feeling well. She told them about the Argus. They told her to take some time off, and she told them she wasn't coming back.

Sarah went to Belgium. She gave a very nice older woman a hug, she got a lifetime's promise of free coffee, and she looked at painting after painting done by people she realized were now dead. She smiled at the nice young woman across the street who sold flowers, and she didn't say hi, but she did wave this time. It was a place to start. Lotte would have wanted something like that.

Flower Crown

Lina was staring at the red star outside her window.

It was a tinted, unblinking thing that watched her from afar. She had often heard that you could make wishes on red stars but she didn't dare make any that night. She held her breath instead and pulled the covers up to her chin.

Gloria, her wet nurse, had already tucked her into bed, but she reveled in the fact she didn't have to go to sleep yet. It was her choice to close her eyes. It was her choice to watch the red night star instead. Besides, Gloria always tucked her into too tightly and forgot to say the bedtime words.

Lina started repeating the words to herself in a singsong voice, "Night, oh night, give us delights in dreams and fairy wings and things that take fli—"

Shuck

Lina bolted upright in bed when the door on the far end of the room swung open. She inhaled softly and searched the darkness for some ghoul from outside the castle grounds. A terrible, rakish creature that supposedly wandered out of the burned wood to suck your blood and munch on your bones. Gloria often repeated stories like that of what happened to bad children in her bedtime tales. Lina clutched the covers more tightly in her small fists and raised them just below her eyes.

"Are you awake, my dear?" A figure shuffled sheepishly into the light, and it was not a ghoul. "I didn't mean to frighten you."

Lina erupted into a wide smile and dropped the blankets

down. "Mommy!" She swung her legs out of bed, but her mom put a hand up.

"I just wanted to check on you." Her mother was still wearing her yellow day dress instead of her pearly white nightgown. Her eyes were slightly shadowed and her shoulders taut. She was a short woman with thick brown corkscrew curls and olive eyes that seemed to hold things in place. Lina believed somewhere in her heart that her mother could hold anything in place with that gaze alone. She could stop floods or cease forest fires with one solid glance.

She had a delicate build and a frowning, small mouth that gave her a look of being perpetually in deep thought. She had a pronounced nose and a smart, round chin that both resembled Lina's own, though Lina's hair grew in thick, wavy bushels instead of the sleek curls of her mother's. They regarded each other for a moment as if waiting for something, and Lina squirmed in place.

Her mother exhaled through her nose. She smiled, and it transformed her face into something younger and sweeter. "How was your day?" She crossed the room and knelt by Lina's bed. The red star glowed just above her head.

"Good," Lina said breathlessly. "I did my letters with Gloria, and then we went outside, and I tried to make mud pies out in the fields before she stopped me."

"Good, good." Her mother reached for her, but her fingers never seemed to find Lina.

Lina frowned and shied away. "Where were you? It was picnic day." They rarely ever got to do picnic day. Lina already knew that.

"I was . . ." Her mother pinched her lips together as if undoing a particularly tangled knot with her mind. "I'm sorry," she said instead. "We'll try again next time."

Lina nodded, but not happily. "Can you tuck me into bed?" she asked in a small voice and snuggled into the covers. It felt indulgent to get tucked in twice, but no one had to know.

"Of course." Mom's eyes were unfocused. She must've forgotten. She must have been engrossed with her own internal world or nascent regrets or maybe just some bad tuna she had for lunch. She thoughtlessly bent down; her hair tickled Lina's forehead for a moment before her lips graced her forehead. She kissed her goodnight.

The reaction was instant. A feeling like when you sit on your arm wrong and it goes numb sprung up through her forehead. It was like static and a twisting wrongness all through her skin, mounting up to that single point.

Her mom's eyes went wild and larger than silver dollar coins. A cold numbness worked its way from the tip of Lina's nose to the end of her ears. Her mouth fell open, but she couldn't make a sound. The feeling extended outside of herself, staticky and strange.

She reached up desperately toward it, but her mother swatted Lina's hand down. "No," she said quickly. "Don't touch it." There was a high-pitched strain in her voice.

"Mommy," she whined. The strangeness extended, and she grasped for it helplessly, her fingers brushing against something rough and rustling. "Mama!" she yelled as leaves and petals manifested from her face and she gasped.

Her eyes started to sting; the numbness was already fading, but there was a bright yellow flower sprouting from her head. "Sssh." Her mother stroked her hair, and her eyes were shining too. "Don't look at it."

Lina started to sniffle more loudly; fat, wet tears rolled down her cheeks as she tried to reach for her mother again. Her mom hesitated for a moment, just a moment.

She picked her up and cradled her close to her chest. "Hush now." Her voice cracked. "This will pass." She clutched her close, pressing Lina's face into her warm shoulder.

"*Ow*." Lina struggled in her arms. The grip was too tight.

"You're safe," her mom said without letting go. Lina sniffled, and when she pulled away, the bright yellow chrysanthemum soundlessly fell to the ground as quickly as it sprouted. It softly settled in a dry bunch on the stone floor and left her face clear and unmarked. Lina's breath hiccupped, and she wiped her cheeks with both hands.

"A flower."

"It's nothing," her mom said in a hush and quickly kicked it away as if it were a dead animal on the floor. "Go to sleep now." Her mom did not lean down to tuck her in this time. She roughly pulled the covers up, and her soft footsteps faded to the other side of the room like a fog rolling away.

Lina turned her face up to the red star, gritted her teeth, and made a wordless, desperate wish. She glanced at the cut flower kicked across the room, and her heart clenched in her chest. She knew at that moment there was something deeply wrong with her.

∞∞∞

Lina was staring at an enormous black bear. Its teeth were yellowed, and the canines were longer than her pointer fingers. Its eyes were dark, glistening holes, and it was reared back as if to attack. She studied the creature's paws the size of her head and its ferocious posture. *Did it have any cubs?* she wondered. *Did it like honey?*

"Ellina!" a voice like cavernous echoes called. A tall, upright man with solid proportions waved for her. "We're walking now, child."

Her father was a sturdy, middle-aged man with dark eyes, a short black beard, and wavy hair that rolled down his shoulder-tops. He was majestic in the way storm clouds were majestic and angry in the same way. Right then he was directing that thunderclap in her direction as she had stopped in front of the stuffed bear in the grand hall.

"Coming." She hurried forward.

Her mom was studying her with that same discerning gaze that remained unreadable even as Lina grew older. Her mom sighed. It was rare to have them all together, but it didn't truly feel like they were. Her parents hastened her along before dipping their heads back together in conversation.

"Did you talk to the stable master?" Her father was curt and waspish.

"I told him simply to prepare a pony," her mom said back calmly. "I don't want any suspicions arising if I give commands that are out of the ordinary . . ."

Their voices melted together into a colorful soup. Lina yawned and strode ahead of them. "Can I go outside already?" she asked without applying any "please" or "thank you" kind of words because that was the easiest way to get their attention.

They both glanced at her before her father pinched the bridge of his nose like he wanted to stop a nosebleed. "Can't this wait?" he said, but not to her.

"She'll be nine in no time." Her mother sounded affronted. "No woman in my family has ever waited this long . . ."

"That's *your* family." They continued to bicker, and Lina groaned before heading toward the double doors.

"You already promised I could go outside today!" She ignored the guards at the doors and went for the handles. They were enormous brass ones that were cool to the touch, even in summer.

"Lina," her mom said harshly. "Lina, one moment."

Her parents seemed to finish their argument with a series of head bobs and short, hissed whispers. Her father quickly melted away to go do some of his *duties* or to re-brush his hair or re-shine his boots or whatever it was her father did when he was away. He was away often.

Her mother, however, caught up to her and took her hand. She had the guards open the double doors for them, and she exhaled slowly in a way Lina knew meant that she was steadying herself. "Come on." Lina tugged on her mom's wrist, and they were out onto the castle grounds and into the streaming buckets of sunshine.

Her mom stumbled forward. "Don't pull, darling."

"I want to see my horse!" She beamed. "You said it was today."

"It is, yes," her mom said, and she gave the smallest of pleased smiles. "He's been waiting for you."

That made Lina light up. "You promised he'd be a palomino."

"You'll just have to wait and see, won't you?" Her mom walked in step with her. They swung their arms back and forth, and it was a deliciously bright day in summer. The grasses were thick with sweetness, and the wind smelled of baking earth. They were outside the castle walls and toward the stables with only a few strides.

Lina was all but buzzing. "I'm thinking of calling it Lord Georgia, for Queen Georgia, the warrior one."

"It's a stallion, darling. A boy horse," her mom said absently. "And it already has a name."

"I *like* the name Georgia for a boy."

Her mom shook her head fondly as they arrived near a dusty round field with a tall wooden pole in the center and an upright fence enclosing the whole thing. An enormous barn sat off to the side, and a young man waved at them as they approached.

Her mother tightened her grip on Lina's hand.

"Oh," Lina murmured as she studied the stranger and looked toward her mom for guidance, "the stable master?"

"Good morning, Your Majesties!" the young man boomed and hopped over the fence to join them. "I've been expecting you."

Like many people in her kingdom, he had licorice-dark hair and deep-set eyes. His chin was boxy, and his shoulders were very square, too, which gave him the look of someone made of more cube than man. He smiled boyishly at the two of them and was the type of person who could have easily been aged anywhere between twenty and thirty-five. He gave them both a deep bow. "Good morning, Princess Ellina."

Lina giggled. She rarely got to see anyone on the castle

grounds, so she rarely had anyone bowing to her. "Hello," she said, "um, you."

"This is Byron," her mother explained and took a step as if to separate the two of them. "He will be teaching you to ride today."

Lina bounced on her heels. "Can I do a jump?" She tugged on her mother's skirts. "I want to do a jump like at the fair." Lina remembered the sticky heat and overly roasted meats of the fair, but more than that, she remembered the dancing horses and carnival acts. The painted white horses had been her favorite.

"You'll have to start with staying *on* the horse," her mom said, not without a smidge of humor laced underneath.

"Byron, sir," Lina turned to the young man, "I'd like to jump today."

He chuckled good-naturedly. "Of course! A princess like you? You're made for jumps. But I'm afraid you'll have to learn the basics first."

Lina found herself nodding enthusiastically. "I can do that!" She let go of her mother's skirts in order to rush forward. Her mother tsked.

"Be careful," she warned before stepping back. "You know the rules."

Lina looked over her shoulder with an irritated huff. "I know the rules."

Byron led her inside to meet her pony. The barn had rows and rows of horses tucked away in stalls in a huge room that smelled musty with hay. Her pony was a sandy, squat animal named Buttercup with white knees and a pale-yellow mane and tail.

"He's been specifically bred for you, Princess," Bryon informed her before teaching her the basics of rubbing down a horse with a brush and putting on a saddle. Lina could barely lift the saddle herself, but she promised herself she would get strong enough soon.

She learned how to squeeze her thighs around the animal

and how to hold the reins. Byron was leading her around in circles outside soon enough and Buttercup walked along at an ambling, slow pace.

"Can't I make him turn myself?" Lina found herself complaining. It was getting hot now, and she wasn't sure if she had learned to ride a horse yet in the least bit.

"You want to try on your own, huh?" Byron said with a smile that stored too much humor inside of its nooks and crannies. "And what will I do if the horse runs away with you?"

Lina sighed dramatically. "Replace me with a decorative housecat, perhaps?"

Byron tossed his head back and laughed. "And what will your family replace *me* with then?"

"A different housecat," she said mischievously. "But one that is more stubborn."

"Two more laps," he said. "And then I'll let you lead."

Lina waited patiently as she was walked around in circles twice more. She held tightly onto the reins when Bryon finally handed them to her. "Remember what I said." His tone became serious for a moment. "Tug gently on the bit to get him to turn."

Lina sat up straight. "I can do that!" She cheered and then kicked the pony to go forward.

"Gently, Princess!" Bryon said as he backed up and Buttercup started to walk more quickly around the ring. "Good. Now turn."

Practice was slow. It took time to get her hands to feel correct on the reins and get used to sitting completely straight in the smooth saddle. Nonetheless, it only took her one more turn to start getting her pony to do laps.

"I'm doing it!" she cheered as the animal sped up. "I'm riding!" They were barely going fast enough to catch spit in the wind, but it was something.

Byron leaned on the fence and waved at them. He was a Floyd, a family that had served her family for generations and lived on the castle grounds. The Floyds all seemed to have a gentle air to them and a genial manner. "Come in now, Princess!" he finally bade her.

Lina's muscles complained, and her skin was sticky with sweat. She was beaming, though. It was nice to learn something new. It was nice to talk to someone new. She reluctantly walked the pony back toward the stables.

"Next time," she proclaimed, "I'm going to do a jump like they do at the fairs—all the way over the fence."

"I'm sure you will." Byron came up next to her. "You'll have all the knights following you in no time."

Lina felt a rush of affection for the young man. People rarely suggested Lina could do much other than get in trouble and be cloistered inside.

"You'll have to be my first one," she sang. "The Buttercup Knight. Named for my horse."

"Of course. Buttercups are my favorite." He reached for her to help her down. "Though you'll have to accept a sad knight who spends all his time shoveling manure."

She laughed, and it made her chest ache somehow. "You'll be my favorite knight, no question!"

"And you'll be my favorite lady, no question."

She put her hand out like a small queen as she had seen her mother do at carnivals and events and for foreign dignitaries. "I'll be Lady Knight Lina," she said and swung her legs around on the horse's back to face him. "And you'll be Knight Byron."

"Lady Lina? I think not." He took her hand as a knight would. "You'll be queen."

He kissed her knuckles playfully to complete their game. Lina's face froze mid-giggle at their antics. The sensation spread before she could even register the touch itself. The blood drained from her face, and the static spread from the center of her chest outward.

"Princess?" a high-pitched voice whispered.

It occurred in a surreal flash. She had forgotten about this. She had hoped to always forget about it. Before she could even cry out, a twig burst from her knuckles in a frenzy of numbness, and leafy greens sprouted all at once. White petals unfurled, and the bush sprouted from her hand with the eagerness of hunger itself. It lunged toward the sun before stopping. The plant hung in the air, both Lina and Byron's faces slack-jawed and empty.

"What—?" The question bit through the air with a certain ferocity.

"Byron!" Lina shouted as the plant finished growing and she pulled away from it with all the force in her small body. She caught a glimpse of the stable master's wide-eyed shock before she went tumbling backward. "Mommy!" she yelled even more loudly before she hit the ground with a hard *thunk* and a shock of pain up her shoulder.

Lina clutched at her now-empty hand as she lay in a halo of petals and wilting leaves that she had created herself. She stared emptily at the seamless blue skies and remembered why she had been hidden away in the castle for all these years in the first place.

Lina watched out her bedroom window. The sun was a bloody laundry basket of colors folding into themselves on the horizon. She could make out the wagons and horses and people on foot walking off the castle grounds and into the low lights. It had only taken a day for the orders to take effect.

Lina leaned on her chin as she watched the procession march out. She set her jaw and twisted toward her mother, who sat upright and unseeing behind her. "He didn't hurt me." It sounded like a whine. "He really didn't hurt me."

Despite her words, Lina's left arm was in a sling where she had landed on it wrong from falling off the pony. Her mother continued to look off into the distance. Lina tried to hop down from her window seat to get her mom's attention.

"It was an accident." She was almost wailing now.

Her mother clasped her hands together. "We meant to do this earlier," she said blankly. "It's a necessary precaution."

Lina stared down at her shoes.

There would be no more stable boys after this. The kitchen staff was reduced. The king's men and their squires were restricted to certain areas of the castle. Lina glanced back out the window, where their staff was lugging bags and knapsacks off into what might as well have been the abyss.

She frowned. "I don't like this," she said, finally articulating the cloyingly sick feeling in her gut. "Mommy, I don't think —"

"It's necessary," her mother declared before sweeping to her feet. She met Lina's eyes with a firmness there. "No one must ever know you are cursed." She turned to leave. "You'll never rule if they find out."

"Why not?" Lina whispered, but she heard no answer as her mother glided out of the room and the click of the lock followed in her wake. Lina put her head back on the windowsill and watched as Byron and every other male staff member was dismissed. She squeezed her eyes shut and turned away from the window. "Fine," she hissed. "It's not like I want flowers sprouting from my skin either."

She dug in her drawers until she found small silk gloves that covered her all the way up past the elbow. She started wearing them throughout her days and sometimes into the nights as well.

∞∞∞

Lina's footsteps echoed through the long hallways splashed with buttery afternoon light. It was late summer and only a few days after her twelfth birthday. The party itself had been a dreary, endless affair of adults telling her how big she had gotten. Today felt like a better birthday, as she could still hear her favorite present: Gloria's soft snores as Lina made her escape. By now she knew her way to the east side of the castle without being spotted. She ducked and wove through the outer halls until the windows grew cracked and a faint breeze wafted up through the floors.

Two little bodies twitched in her hands. It had been a pain to keep them in her room that whole afternoon without her tutors noticing. She had had to cough twice into her hands when they chirped too loudly, and her embroidery mistress paused in her lessons.

Lina made a turn into a long hall with windows the size of doors. None of them had glass, and they let in a thick and heady breeze. A courtyard stood on the other side, which was overgrown with weeds, long grasses, and tall beech-trees. Broken stone steps led down into its depths, and it had a strangely lonely feel to it. The east wing of the castle had been cleared out and abandoned for as long as Lina had been alive.

She grinned at a series of sticks that were still in place on the hallway floor. They were built up to be as tall as her pinky finger and spanned almost half the length of the space. It had taken them an entire morning to build the racetrack days before. Lina scuffed her foot on the castle stones.

"Mary!" she called out. "Mary, I'm here!"

She huffed when she heard no reply. Lina walked around in circles until the sun became slanted and rosy through the large windows. She eyed the end of the hall and waited for Gloria to wake up and come spitting and fussing down the way. She would bark about how Lina was late—late for lessons, late for meals, late for everything.

Lina started grumbling at her feet. "I'm leaving if you don't show up, Mary!" It was an empty threat.

It was almost two minutes later when she finally heard someone's steps thwacking on the floor and short wheezy gasps of breath. A dark-haired, willowy girl came crashing around the corner. "I'm here!"

Mary Floyd appeared with her cheeks flushed as golden ripe apples and her hands waving above her head. She was a tall girl with wide shoulders, knobby-knocking knees that reminded Lina of clumsy puppies, and long raven hair that swept down her back in a thick braid. She wore an undyed brown dress with grease stains on the front and a white apron that was slung across her shoulder. Her eyes were set deep into her face, and she had a lovingly round cherry nose. She carried a small wooden cage at her hip, and she was grinning like a daybreak.

"I'm here," she repeated after catching her breath. "Phew. Were you waiting long?"

"Yes," Lina said sharply. "I barely finished my numbers in time to get here."

Mary blew a stray piece of hair out of her face. "Mama had me scrubbing the big pots this afternoon." She shook her head. "No helping it."

Two crickets chirped from inside the tiny cage at her waist. Lina glanced at them and noted how they looked bigger than her own. She adjusted her grip on her crickets. "Does that take long?"

"Longer than you might think." Mary started walking toward their makeshift racing tracks.

"At least they let you wander off after," Lina noted sullenly.

"Yeah. After nine big pots! I swear, all of you must eat a horse a day." Mary scoffed loudly and unhooked the cage from her side.

"Who would eat a horse?" Lina blinked a couple times. "Anyway, I'd love to run around like you do. It's way more fun."

Mary rolled her eyes in an exaggerated manner. She held her cage up. "Don't be bitter, Princess," she said with a toothy grin. "You'll make our little friends here slower!"

"I told you." Lina rounded the stick track herself. "That's a silly theory. Crickets don't understand us. They don't have ears like we do."

Mary gave a laugh like a thunderclap—booming and beyond herself. "That's what you think!" she sang and held up her little cage. She poked the bigger cricket inside. "You guys are winners! You hear me? Winners."

Lina couldn't help but snicker herself. "You're just scaring

THE SOFT LANDING COLLECTION

them."

"Maybe." Mary knelt down with her cage in tow. "But we'll see who's right in the end."

They worked together to fix the sticks perfectly in place for the race itself. They took their perch at the starting line and eyed each other as they readied themselves. Lina held her racers loosely in each palm, and Mary reached for the small latch on the cage.

They glanced at each other. "Don't cry when I win," Mary taunted. Her eyes were glowing a fiery amber in the late light of the sun.

"You wish! I'll only be crying tears of joy for my victory," Lina said with her stubborn chin in the air, and Mary just giggled.

"Ready?" She nodded and they started to chant together.

"One, two . . ." They exchanged a gleeful look. "Three!"

They threw their hands in the air and released the insects in a frenzy of movement and sharp little voices. Lina's first cricket skittered backward immediately off the track. One of Mary's bugs jumped sideways and was lost to them in the long gloomy halls of the east wing. They managed to coax the other two racers forward with their hands.

"Go, Mustard Seed, go!" Mary cheered. "Eyes on the prize."

"You named it Mustard Seed?" Lina laughed. "Oh my God."

"Mustard Seed, you're a winner! Don't listen to the naysayers." Mary whooped and pumped her fist in the air. The crickets were careening down the little path now toward the empty finish line.

Lina turned to her fighter. "Go, Cricket Number One, go!"

They were shouting ridiculously at the insects as they neared the end, the crickets pitching toward the finish line and Mary and Lina hooting and clapping their hands. Mustard Seed came across the line in two enormous hops before Cricket Number One did.

"You saw that!" Mary hopped back to her feet and jabbed a finger in the air. "You totally saw that."

"Oh, come on." Lina hung her head.

"My way works." Mary spun around in a circle.

Lina crossed her arms over her chest. "You've been feeding them nice kitchen food, I bet. That's cheating."

"Nuh-uh." Mary turned to her. "I got them out of my yard this morning, just like you did. Fair is fair." She did a small victory dance in place.

"Fiiine," Lina said with a groan and relented. She grumbled to herself for a minute or so before Mary started making faces at her. They got busy catching the remaining crickets they could find and fitting them in their hands again. Mary led the way toward the stone steps that fed into the abandoned east courtyard. As the castle had expanded and been renovated, this section had been forgotten and thus claimed by two wayward girls who should have never known each other in the first place. Lina secretly felt profoundly lucky that she had run into the other girl on her ninth birthday at all. She felt even more lucky that something had stuck between them.

They went down the steps and knelt to release the crickets back into the grass. The girls exhaled slowly like deflated cushions as they sat back onto the stone steps and watched the sun capsize into the tree line. Lina's skin prickled as Mary's eyes landed on her.

She tried to shrug it off and keep her attention fixed on the sky slowly fading into a layered, creamy blackness.

"Hey," Mary finally said as her eyes still itched across Lina's neck, "Princess?"

Lina frowned slowly and turned to her. "You don't have to call me that," she said with a strange shifting on her insides. "Lina is fine."

"What? No, that's not allowed," Mary said quickly and kicked her legs out. "Who even calls you that?"

"Gloria does," Lina said petulantly, "when we're alone."

"We're definitely not allowed to do that. Definitely not," Mary said cheekily and leaned in close to her, "Lina."

Lina couldn't help herself and started beaming. This was

what she liked about Mary. They were rarely allowed such long playtimes together, and it felt like sucking on a candy until your tongue turned a different color. Lina was sure she was all sorts of different colors inside when she was with Mary.

"Not allowed to at all," Mary sang.

Lina held Mary's gaze for a long second before shyly casting her eyes downward. "There's plenty of things we're not allowed to do anyway."

Mary hummed and scooted closer to her. "What exactly can't a *princess* do?" She emphasized the word "princess" with great strain in each syllable.

Lina turned her face away and scowled at the greenery in front of them. "Lots of things. You know that."

"Like the boy thing?" Mary said quietly in bold tones. "Everybody whispers about that."

Lina curled into herself like a dried autumn leaf. "You're not supposed to," she said tightly.

"My brother worked in the stables," Mary said without any brightness to her words. "He's gone now. Do you hate boys? Is that why my brother had to leave?"

Lina picked her head up. "I don't hate boys." She snickered. "I barely know them!"

Mary chuckled lowly, too, though her gaze was deadly serious. "They're not all that great," she said jovially. "All my younger brothers do is whine and make me do the dishes." She huffed. "As if I don't do enough dishes already!"

Lina offered her a small smile and uncurled slightly. "I've never had any siblings," she said in a low voice. "I don't think my mom wants any more."

"Is that why you made my brother get another job?" Mary asked testily. "Because the queen doesn't want any more sons around?"

Lina sensed a great divide yawning between them and creating a stark darkness in their midst. Lina desperately wanted to bridge that gap.

"No," she said and picked at the hem of her dress. "That's

not it." Her thoughts bounced around in her head like slippery objects she couldn't get her hands on. She hunched her shoulders. "That's not it at all."

"What is it then?" Mary pressed. Her little face was still scrunched up in irritation.

Lina looked up and away. "It's a secret."

"What?" Mary gave a brisk laugh. "Like an oath-to-God, full-blown secret?"

Lina twisted her mouth to the side. "Mommy says I can't tell anyone." She knocked her knees together and leaned back to look at the stars popping out one by one. "It's why she won't get too close to me, I guess."

"Huh?" Mary's eyes grew wide. She inched closer to her to the point they were almost touching, and Lina tingled down her spine for it. "Why? Is she afraid of you?"

Lina made a small noise in the back of her throat. "I dunno. Probably," she said hesitantly. She bit her bottom lip. She tried not to think about this. "You'd be afraid of me, too, if you knew. It's not . . . normal."

Mary bumped their knees together. "No way," she said lightly. "I wouldn't be afraid of you. I'm taller than you. I could pick you up and throw you if I wanted to, Princess."

Lina frowned and primly tucked a piece of her hair behind her ear. "Mary, it's not funny. It's scary. People are scared of me."

"I wouldn't be." Mary lifted her chin proudly in the air. "I take the big spiders outside when no one else wants to."

Lina balled her skirts up in her fists. She gnashed her teeth in frustration. "It'd freak you out just like everyone else."

"Bet it wouldn't." Mary sat up straight and looked directly at Lina. "Bet it wouldn't scare me one lick."

"Bet it would," Lina challenged back darkly.

"I bet," Mary said, poking her shoulder, "I'm braver than you think."

Lina set her jaw and turned to her. "They got rid of all the boys in the castle because if anyone kisses me, they . . ." She searched the air for the right words to describe it. "They . . ."

Mary leaned in close and hissed, "Do you die?" She reached for Lina's hand to squeeze it. "Do *they* die?"

Lina shook her head and tried to ignore the heat rising in her face. Mary's hand lay over hers. "This thing happens," she tried to explain. "It comes out of my skin. It's . . . bad."

"What comes out?" Mary was a breath away from her now, and she was practically vibrating in place. "Like toads and snakes?"

Lina raised her eyebrows. "No, no," she said and gestured. "Like plants. Flowers."

A long moment passed after her declaration. She had said it. She had admitted to the one thing she shouldn't. Lina held her breath and quaked inside like a leaf about to be snatched into a tempest. Mary blinked rapidly, and her entire face was blank. Finally, the mask broke clean away, and she started snickering. "Flowers?" She laughed with her shoulders shaking. "Flowers come out?"

She dissolved into a full-blown giggle fit.

Lina stomped her foot on the ground. "It's not funny!" she defended. "Mommy says it's dangerous." She tried to make it clear to Mary as everyone else had to her.

Mary covered her mouth, but her shoulders didn't stop shaking. "I thought you were gonna say *die*, Lina."

Lina's face flushed. She looked down at her feet. "Everyone hates curses," she said slowly. "You've heard about what they did to the Justinian Princess."

Mary stopped laughing and tilted her head to the side. She reached out without a hint of shame and pushed a bushel of Lina's hair back. "Curse? Yours doesn't sound like a curse, not even a little."

Lina pouted. "Gloria is afraid of me. Mommy won't come near me. My father doesn't even want to see me." The words flooded out of her like water out of a newly made hole in a bucket. "Everyone thinks . . . they think," she mumbled. "They think I'm tainted. Wrong." She remembered the word *tainted* from one of her parents' many hushed conversations about her. "Don't you get it?"

"It sounds . . . not terrible," Mary murmured. "I mean, flowers? Kinda nice. Romantic." She sighed dreamily. "You could give them to a lover."

Lina wrinkled her nose. "Gross!"

"What's it feel like?" Mary turned to her and examined her as if she were a whole different beast now.

"It kinda just goes numb," Lina said slowly. She had never tried to explain it before. "And twists." She hummed. "But it hasn't happened in a while. And it *is* a curse!" she insisted. "No one is allowed to like me. It's forbidden."

"Well," Mary said and pressed their shoulders together, "it's already too late, because I like you."

"No, you don't," Lina snapped back at her. "You're just saying that."

Mary huffed. "You think I run down halls for just anyone? You're, like, so much more fun than the other kids. The others won't even catch crickets with me anymore."

Lina sucked on her bottom lip. She turned away. "Well, you're breaking the rules then. No kisses. No flowers."

Mary puffed her chest out and pointed at herself. "I'm not afraid of flowers." She snorted. "No one's afraid of flowers."

"And what if they stab you?" Lina said decidedly.

"Doing what?" Mary bounced in place.

Lina blew hot air out of her nose. "With, you know, the kiss."

Mary tugged on her sleeve to get her attention. Her dark eyes were large and shiny. "Me?" she said with a look of awe. "You'd let me see it? I'd love to see the flower thing."

Lina pulled away. "You don't actually like me." Her face was too hot all of the sudden, and her chest filled with tiny pinpricks like thorns.

Mary abruptly grabbed her face between her calloused hands. She turned Lina's face toward her. "Bet I do," she whispered hoarsely. "I bet I like you tons."

Lina chuckled tensely, and the nerves of her body were alight like burst sparklers. "No," she said slowly, "you can't."

"Too bad."

Mary started to draw closer. She licked her chapped lips, and everything inside Lina ground to a halt. No more breathing. No more moving. Just her heart hammering away in her chest.

"You'll be weirded out," she defended.

Mary was closing in. Her mischievous grin had faded, and she tapped their foreheads together lightly. Her skin was warm and thrumming with life. "You're already pretty weird." Lina could smell the scent of dish soap on her. She was so close. "Can't get any weirder now, Princess."

"Princess?" Lina wrinkled her nose. "I thought you wanted to see the flower thing."

Mary gulped, and she was barely a hair away. Her eyes were caverns of expression and movement. "Lina then," she said softly.

Lina nodded at her, and it barely took a second.

She closed the gap between them in one swift motion of clumsy boldness. It felt like running headlong into a freezing lake without a stitch of clothing on. It felt like hurrying her horse into a canter with a blindfold on. She screwed her eyes shut and gripped at Mary's shoulders tightly.

Mary's mouth was firm and real against hers for just a moment. It was brief and electric and made something sing and swoop in her chest. It was only the finest moments of relief.

Something curled out of her face like it was yanked out of somewhere deep within her. It pushed its way outward in a numb frenzy. Lina's eyes watered, and she peered out at something enormous. The side of her mouth was staticky and almost painful.

"Ah!" she cried out and clawed at her face as an entire rosebush pushed outward. Four blood-red roses unfurled at an unnatural speed, and their perfect petals were scattered with the last of the speckled sunshine.

"Lina!" Mary crowed. "That's beautiful!"

She tried to cover it with her hands weakly. "It's gonna eat me."

Mary reached out and touched one of the flowers in wonder. "You're like a human garden."

"Don't be mean, Mary."

Mary grabbed her shoulder and squeezed. "It's lovely." She grinned widely, "It's—"

"Princess! Was that you?" a new voice called at them. "Where have you been? What are you . . ." The words died in the nursemaid's mouth. Both of their heads jerked in the direction of a stout woman with snow-white hair and a stricken expression.

The flowers started to fall just as quickly as they appeared, and a hollow, terrible feeling settled in Lina's gut. "I have to go now," she said woodenly as she stared at Gloria. Gloria had seen the flower sprouting from her lips. She had seen everything. "*You* need to go now."

"Why?" Mary stared at her. "I'll tell them, Lina. I'll tell them it's not dangerous. I'll tell them it's fine! I'll let them know to stop worrying."

Lina shook her head weakly, and Gloria finally spoke. Her lips curled back in a snarl. "What have you done?"

Lina knew it was over then.

Bang, bang, bang. The door rattled on its hinges.

Lina's pillowcase was soggy, and everything was salt and tight-throated sorrow. "You can't do this! You can't do this!" she wailed without thought to decency or volume. "It wasn't her fault."

"Lina!" Gloria and her mother rattled the door handle again. "Open up right now."

"It isn't fair!" she roared in response, and a big burbling sob built up in her chest anew. "It's not right! Bring her back."

She kicked her feet into her mattress and almost screamed.

Her father's voice cut above the fray. "Ellina, listen to your mother. This is no time for childish fits." She hadn't taken food for the entire day now and had locked the door from the inside out. "The castle is already talking. We must show a unified front. We must show some normalcy."

Bang, bang, bang.

"She was my only friend . . ." Lina was surprised she had any more tears left as they ran down her cheeks in a messy stream. She sniffled pathetically. "You can't send her away!"

The Floyds were gone. Mary was gone. She could barely swallow the thought, much less live with it.

"You think we *wanted* to dismiss a family that's been at this castle for generations?" Her father was blunt and sterile in speech. "No one wants to deal with curses, child. No one wants to bend to the curse's will, but it was the only way."

"Deal with curses? Deal with it?" she shrieked and picked up her pillow to throw it at the door. "You're not the one who has to live with it!" The pillow bounced off the wall uselessly, and she threw herself against the mattress anew. Something was burrowing deep inside of her and festering.

They sent away her only friend, and she didn't even get to say goodbye. Lina wasn't sure she was going to be the same after that.

$$\infty\infty\infty$$

The pantry door swung shut behind her, and Lina quickly lowered the latch. The dinnertime bell was ringing nearby with an obnoxious clang. There was a visiting dignitary come to call that night. There was an after-dinner tea she had to attend. There was small talk to be had and eye contact to be demurely avoided.

She stared at a wooden door and inhaled the scents of dry flour and salted meats. Something itched underneath Lina's skin like a blanket made of thistles. She was fourteen that year and wanted to scream. She had stopped talking to her mother. She only had barbs to offer her father. She was *ready* to scream.

She ripped off her long periwinkle gloves and rolled her bell-shaped sleeves up past the elbow. Her eyes bore holes into her bare skin, and she started to grumble to herself.

"Don't go outside, Lina," she mimicked sharply. "No one can know, Lina. Don't look at any boys, Lina." She snorted loudly at the last note. "Stop sulking, Lina. It was only a scullery maid."

Her hands shook, and her belly was bursting with a suppressed fury. She was not going to be conversing with any visiting dignitaries that evening.

"All right." She steadied herself. "You're already born bad, Lina.... Let's see how bad you can actually get."

She scowled at the pantry door for another moment like it personally offended her. Finally, she dove down in a single sweeping movement. She bent over and kissed her pointer finger with a jerky touch. Static prickled through her skin, but she accepted it this time. Two twin cherry blossoms shot out of her with thick wooden branches that fell to the floor with a clatter.

She took a deep breath. "Come on now. Show me something nice." She kissed her wrist and the crook of her elbow. Rows of springtime flowers bounded forth—tendrils of snapdragons and purple blossoms that smelled of honey. She kissed across her other arm and watched as blood-red anemone, fragrant hyacinth, buttercups, larkspur all riddled her skin.

She peppered every inch of her she could touch with small, brief kisses. She covered herself in an automatic garden that sprouted and fell away like passing seasons. *Tainted,* they said, *a fairy's touch. A cursed girl.*

She brought hydrangea, lilies, and daffodils to life with only her body and a pain now sizzling through her system. The entire floor around her was littered with petals and fallen foliage. Flowers she couldn't name burst forth, and her limbs grew heavy and numb as stones, but she didn't care. She wanted to know.

"Princess Ellina!" someone called.

Lina muttered the only curse word she knew as she heard someone storming into the kitchen at a clipped pace.

"Where is my daughter?" her mother asked in a hardened, flat tone.

Lina knelt down onto the floor as if to hide and kissed a dahlia out of her wrist. She hissed at the pain—it was getting worse with each flower.

"I'm not sure," an unsteady voice answered her mom. It was Chrissy, the red-haired, big-eyed kitchen girl. She must've entered the room while Lina was busy.

"Lina!" Her mother was no fool as she called into the air. "Lina, come out here! We've checked the rest of the grounds. There's no need to hide like this."

Lina huffed and kissed an entire sunflower out of her shoulder before standing up again. She drew a deep breath. "In here, mother." Her voice didn't even shake as she said it.

Clicking heels approached followed by a harsh gasp. She must have seen the fallen flower petals seeping out of the crack under the door.

"What have you done?" The question lacked all heat.

Lina tore open the pantry door and stood tall. Her nostrils flared, and she could already see her mother's face contorting at the spectacle.

"What have *I* done?" Lina repeated with vehemence. She tried to keep her scowl trained and brutal as her mother faced her. "Everything you've ever told me to," she said with a wicked grin. "And now the opposite."

Her mother turned around in one fluid motion. "Christina," she addressed the terrified kitchen help, "get everyone out of the kitchen vicinity, now, or you will be dismissed."

Chrissy gave a sloppy curtsey and scrambled to leave the room. She went to address the rest of the kitchen staff, who were mostly congregated in the other room. She hurried them out with a few unheard words and left Lina alone with her mother's blizzard. The sunflower fell to the floor between them, and that's where it stayed.

"You don't know what you've done," her mother said bloodlessly.

Lina ground her teeth down. "I never do," she hissed back. "And why, Mom? Because I'm poisoned? It's flowers, Mom. Flowers!" she insisted.

Her mom bent down and scooped up a handful of daffodils. She held them out between them. "And who do you think is going to trust a queen with plants growing out of her? With a fairy's touch? They'd run us out. Plus . . ." She left the sentence hanging there like a dead thing.

Lina screwed her face up. "Then what happened, Mom? Why did you make me like this?!" She stomped her foot as more flowers shook off her clothing and rained down dead leaves and petals to the floor.

Her mom's shoulders fell, and she grimaced. Defeat was written across her face in a way Lina didn't want to read. "I didn't." She closed her eyes. "I didn't mean . . ." She drew a deep, shuddery breath. Her frame no longer seemed so looming. She was mortal as she stood before her daughter and shook. She stared at the dead flowers on the floor for a long moment. "We snubbed her. The eastern fairy queen."

Lina wasn't done being angry yet. "So?" She bared her teeth like the stuffed bear in the grand hall. "She gave me flowers? That's it?"

"We didn't know exactly what she did at first," her mom murmured. "I just knew it said my daughter will die as the flowers grow."

Lina's eyes grew wide. "What does that mean?"

Her mom reached for the doorframe to lean on it. "Magic comes at a price." She wouldn't meet her eyes. "I didn't want to scare you with it. You're so young . . . but there it is."

"A price?" She deflated slowly.

Her mother nodded. "One will fade while the other grows."

Lina stood perfectly still. She looked around at the carnage she had created. "You should have told me." She took a step back. "They're—"

"They're draining you." Her mother trembled and leaned more heavily on the door. "You must have heard in your studies. Magic takes and it takes."

A perfect lily trapped in her skirts tumbled to the floor. Lina reared up. "And you didn't tell me what it would take?!" She was in an ocean of her own making. A raft set adrift in a place she barely recognized.

Her mother's mouth was a hard line. "Why? To frighten my only daughter to death?"

"Yes!" Lina threw her hands in the air. "To tell me anything!"

Her mother exhaled slowly. "Wasn't my warning enough?" It was almost gentle. She gave a frail laugh. "I suppose not."

Lina's eyes unfocused and she wilted. "How do I stop it?" she asked in a daze. The flowers were killing her.

The queen lowered her head. "We burned the fairy queen's woods to the ground," she said solemnly, "and she still wouldn't tell us."

Lina's face screwed up. "You did *what*?" She paused and recalled her studies. "You didn't just offer her a gift?"

"Of course we tried that first," her mom snapped back.

Lina leaned forward like a threat. "You burned her place down!"

"I was afraid! Don't you understand?" Her mom's voice was hoarse, and half broken. "It's...it's going to get worse, Lina."

Lina looked at her mutely. Her life-force was scattered around her like a funeral, and she was more alone than she had ever been. She was fourteen, and it seemed screaming hadn't helped.

∞∞∞

"I'm going out riding!" Lina called over her shoulder.

"Come back here right now, young lady." Gloria was getting old with her knees busted out and liver spots appearing on her hands. She hastened to follow Lina out the door. "We're not done discussing what you said to the governess."

Lina rolled her eyes. "It was nothing new." She hurried along without any thought to Gloria keeping pace. "She knows I don't care for her notes on my stitchwork."

Gloria growled in the back of her throat. "Asking her to politely and sincerely kiss your—well. It's unseemly."

Lina shrugged. "When have I ever been seemly?"

"Young lady, you are sixteen now, and you can't go around with such a vulgar tongue."

Lina opened her mouth to demonstrate the full extent of her vulgar tongue and wasn't paying attention. She was looking over her shoulder when she made a sharp turn toward the front doors of the castle.

"Oof!" She collided headlong with a laundry maid carrying a basket of fresh linens. They both toppled to the floor in a heap. Lina's skin brushed against the maid's hand.

She inhaled sharply at the contact and the now familiar feeling: pinpricks of numbness that sprouted all at once. Dark peonies and a single enormous morning glory budded and opened across her collarbone. "Oh no, oh no."

"Princess! I am so sorry," Louise, one the maids, sounded off immediately with a sheet over her face. Lina tried to cover herself before the laundry maid picked herself up and saw royalty turning into foliage. Lina rolled away with new horror churning in her guts.

Gloria stood behind her with her hand outstretched. "What did she do?"

"Nothing." Lina held her numb shoulder as the flowers wilted off onto the floor. Her heart was beating two times too fast. "I have to check on something."

"What? Are you all right?"

"I have to go!" she nearly shrieked and started running.

She watched the corners more carefully as she sprinted away but didn't allow herself to slow. She thought Gloria might come after her, but the old woman just stayed in place and watched her retreat. Lina ran out into the pastures with a slippery panic coating her insides.

She went to Buttercup with his head bowed and his tail flicking in the pastures. "Here boy," she said in a hush, and he lifted his head slowly to greet her. Lina put out her bare hand. She barely grazed his soft velvet nose before her fingers burst with purple asters along her palm. Lina dropped to the ground and curled up into an unbreachable ball.

It wasn't just kisses anymore.

Rain battered against the stained-glass windows with a steady *pit-pit-pit-pit*. Thunder clapped in the distance, and Lina didn't so much as blink with each new strike. The throne room was an enormous, spacious place with a velvet red carpet leading up to three stone chairs built into the floor. The thrones were gray structures with intricate carvings on the legs and soft red cushions placed on each hard surface. Kings and queens before her had sat on these exact seats said to be carved from the mountain her kingdom was founded on long ago.

Lina sat on the throne of the heir with her head held high and her eyes puffy and spent. Her brow was heavy with a golden crown that she struggled to keep upright. It was a little too large for her, and she was only supposed to wear it for ceremonies. She wore it now as another enormous thunderclap boomed outside.

New tears stung her eyes, but she swallowed them readily. Powder-soft footsteps came from the other side of the room. The darkness hid the figure, but she was not so young anymore to think it was a forest ghoul. It was far worse.

Her father stalked into the lights cast from the stained-glass windows and frowned at her. He had crow's feet around his eyes now and bits of silver streaking his beard. He straightened his spine before addressing her. "You shouldn't sit in the dark," he said without preamble. "Come, let's go to your chambers where a fire is burning. It's cold." He was ever the practicalist.

A flash of lightning lit the entire room in stark paleness. Lina lifted her chin higher. "No," she said simply. "I don't think so."

Her father rubbed the back of his neck with one large hand. "There is something we need to discuss with you," he said haltingly. "I was . . . opposed to it at first, but your mother thinks it's best."

Lina leaned back against the cold, hard chair. "So?"

Her father sighed. "Are you really wearing your crown right now? For God's sake, Lina."

She shrugged and looked away. "It might be the last time I get to." She reached up to touch its cool surface. "You both are always saying I'll never be queen with the way I am now. I might as well play pretend for one night."

Her father stared coldly down at the floor with his hands bunched up into fists. "Lina," he said venomously before bowing even lower and exhaling, "we care about you." His voice broke. "We care more than you know."

Lina turned her face toward where the rain was drumming against the windows. "I know," she said, but it sounded like an entirely different set of words.

"And there's still time," her father insisted. "There's more we can do. We still have options."

"If I brush hands with someone at the dinner table," she said loudly in a monotone. "If my chamber maid tries to help me dress. If I want to touch my goddamn horse—"

"Lina!" he said, aghast.

"Then the flowers grow," she said steadily, "and I wither." She stood with a single jerky motion and held her crown in place. "How much longer do you even think I have?"

Her father stopped playing the role of the hapless man

and scowled with a gaze that had little give. "There are still options," he repeated. "There is another castle. The old one. On the outskirts of the kingdom."

"Oh?" she said and crossed her arms over her chest. "So, I can go *there* to die?"

He shook his head. "We have a plan." He strode over toward her with his shoes thudding across the bare stone as he walked off the carpet tread. "We can make it sound sympathetic—like it can be broken. No one has to know where it came from. Though . . . you may have to go away."

"Of course." She reached for her crown and gently took it off her brow. "No one can know." She stood, turned around mechanically, and placed her crown on the cushion. Her father could put it away himself if he wanted to.

"Lina," he insisted, "nothing is lost yet. You are still my heir, and I am not going to let you be laid in the ground before I am."

Lina gave a bitter smile. "That is probably the nicest thing you've ever said to me," she said airily before walking past him and into the darkness beyond. "Though who knows how long you have to keep saying it."

"No!" he said sharply to her back. "Don't speak like that. Don't give up hope yet!"

She cracked the door open as another thunderclap resounded, and she slipped into the hallway and away from her father's hopes and pleas.

∞∞∞

"It's not forever." Her mother gave her a difficult look like milk churning to butter. "We have something we're working on."

Lina was out on the castle grounds, and the scene was a smear of commotion. An entire caravan was being packed up. Her bedspreads and favorite nightgowns and shoes all bundled into cases and put on the backs of horses. *Do I really own all of those shoes?* she pondered for a moment.

"Did you hear me?" Her mother and father were standing together for once. Lina snapped to attention.

"How long?" she asked briskly, and her father gestured for more of her cloaks and blankets to be stored away.

"We have a plan," her mom repeated and started wringing her hands. She had been doing that a lot recently. "It won't be long."

Lina turned to her listlessly. The fight had left her body months ago. "How long is that?"

Her father seemed to notice them for the first time. He turned to his daughter and wife. "We'll be giving you enough nonperishables to last through the winter," he said factually, "and into spring."

"Oh."

"We'll send more when the time arrives," he continued as if he wasn't sending his only daughter away into the unknown.

Lina turned around in circles to search for something. She realized belatedly that there was no one else to say goodbye to. Only her parents, who looked at her with more sorrow than she thought existed in the whole universe.

"We'll write to you." Her mom reached for her before stopping. "We'll write to you and send carrier pigeons every week." Her eyes were shining, and Lina looked away. She watched as they heaved all of the dried meats into a single carriage by the barrel.

Seven months of supplies. Seven months of being sent away. Seven months on her own.

"Gloria will teach you some basic mending and cooking on the way," her mother continued as if Lina was listening. "Your dresses will all be ones you can put on by yourself." Her mother looked like she was holding herself together with the thinnest piece of yarn stretched thin.

"All right. Though I at the very least know how to mend," Lina said sullenly before looking back to where the horses were flicking their ears back and forth. "How far is it again?"

"Three days' ride," her father said without blinking. "You'll be safe. We've surveyed ahead to make sure the path is clear."

Of course it will be clear, Lina thought, not without a hint of melancholy, *because no one lives out in the eastern province in the first place.*

She touched her hair for something to do and studied the wooden carriage that would take her away from the only home she had ever known. She turned back to her parents and knew she couldn't hug them goodbye.

"Well," she said instead, "so long."

Her mother hid her face in her hands for just a moment. The king adjusted his belt as he kept surveying the work. "We'll be back for you," he said loudly. "It won't be long until a solution is found. We'll come get you."

She simply shook her head and got into the carriage with Gloria. She pressed her forehead against the glass and waited for her castle and her old life to disappear in a blur behind her.

∞∞∞

"What do you use for fevers?" The old woman's hands moved fluidly over her work. She was knitting Lina another hat. Lina figured she already had enough hats, but who was she to say? The carriage gave a frightening creak, and Lina sighed.

She scratched her wrist. "Ginger?" she guessed. "And cloves."

Gloria peered up from her work to look ruefully at Lina. "Good enough," she muttered. "What ointments help with rashes?"

Lina leaned toward the window to poke the curtains aside. "Aren't I bringing books along to educate me on this sort of thing? Hopefully, I won't be getting sick at all."

"Come on now, girl. You've had lessons for years."

"Not on medicine." Lina hummed. "I think it was an oatmeal bath?" She glanced toward the enormous trees out the window. They were growing larger, wilder, and more twisted the farther they got out. The roots stuck up from the ground in thick, gnarled tendrils, and the animals grew larger in size and fewer in number. "And I'll have oatmeal with me, I suppose."

"Good, yes." The clicking of Gloria's needles filled the carriage, and her shoulders were taut, and worry lines spread across her wrinkled face. This was the last day of their journey after a hard three days' ride. "And," she said before she drew in a deep breath, "what helps with coughs?" Her voice was getting watery.

"I don't know." Lina rubbed the back of her neck. "Tea? Honey?"

"Yes." Gloria sighed. "Do you even know how to make your own tea?"

Lina shrugged. "I'll figure it out."

Gloria's hands worked more furiously over her hat. "Sending you away like this," she muttered to herself with hot puffs of breath. "Don't even know how to boil your own water."

"It can't be too hard, yeah?" Lina mustered a small smile and looked out the window again. The sky was a smoky gray, and the path rattled and rumbled onward. The smooth stone had given way to this dusty, uneven road a few miles back.

Gloria's needles stopped clicking for a moment. She wiped at her haggard face before looking Lina directly in the eyes. "Take care of yourself," she said like she was reading a commandment from a holy text. "You have to take care of yourself."

Lina reached her hand out to take Gloria's but then remembered herself at the last minute. She settled back into the seat. "It will only be a few months," she said weakly, and she wasn't sure she believed herself. "Besides, I'll finally learn to make my own tea. That'll be good."

"Yes, yes." Gloria went back to knitting. "Bundle up, all right? Do you remember what works best for mumps?"

"No, but I'm sure you'll tell me," Lina said playfully, but then her eyes strayed to the window one last time. A lone tower stuck up from the land like a jagged mountain peak. It was of black charred stone and turrets done in the old fashion with severe points. "There," she said softly. "We're here."

Gloria sucked in a breath before furiously finishing off her hat. "Here." She carefully passed over the lumpy gray wool thing. "Wear this."

It was barely into fall, but Lina tugged on the wool cap and ignored the lump in her throat. "Thank you," she said before she knew she had to get out. When she knew she would have to depart for good. "Thank you," she murmured and pursed her lips together, "for all of it."

Gloria flicked away a single tear and then nodded. "You'll be safe here," she promised, but Lina wasn't even sure that was what she wanted at this point. She pulled aside the curtains and watched the castle tower as if it might speak to her.

"Gloria"—her voice was thin and frail against the rocking carriage—"why is this castle abandoned again?"

Gloria muttered toward her hands for a moment before setting her mouth in a hard line. "You know the answer, girl."

Lina looked past the tower and toward the rolling hills. The land beyond the tower was blackened and populated by the twisting corpses of trees. She nodded coldly at the sight. It was fitting to be left to the wilderness with the burned woods on her doorstep.

"Can't believe they won't even let me come with you," Gloria complained before touching her own hand to the window. "It's unsightly for a princess to live like this . . ."

"I'll manage," Lina said bitterly before letting the curtain fall and the scene of the burned woods just beyond disappear. "I'll have to."

∞∞∞

In the first month, she learned how to boil a pot of water.

In the second month, she learned how to mend her own

rips in her gowns.

In the third month, she learned how true loneliness tasted and started to sing to herself in the hallways. She learned from books how to knead and bake her own bread. Lina was rather proud of that one—no matter how many times she burned the crust.

In the fourth month, it started to snow.

The rooms of the castle were drafty and large. They looked like they were meant to house at least thirty people at a time in drawing rooms and various bedrooms and the ballroom. It was a vast and unsorted kind of place. It reminded Lina of what living with ghosts might feel like: an abandoned spindle here, a stray pot there, and so many spiderwebs to be kicked apart. There was never any end to the tasks to be completed and things to be scrubbed and rooms to be cleared off. It kept her busy.

It was late one night when she stopped. The wind howled against the shudder of a window, and Lina huddled under two blankets with her fire spitting and burning away in the room's hearth. She was in a master bedroom with a big dusty feather mattress in the center of it and creaky wooden chairs positioned around the fireplace. It would have been homey if not for the crumbling doorway and long shadows playing games across the walls.

Lina was singing her old bedtime song to herself in order to ignore the bristling snowstorm outside. "Night, oh night, give us delights in dreams and fairy wings and things that take flight. I fancy your stars and fancy your moon. Oh, where do you go when the sunlight blooms? Oh, where do you go with my dreams and my fears? Night, oh night—"

Something twisted in the shadows by the wall. Lina turned around swiftly.

"Hello?" Her voice sounded faint to her own ears. There was a shadow on the wall. She pulled her blankets tighter around her shoulders and reached for something to throw. "Is anyone—"

The shadow darted away, and Lina followed it with her eyes. A small smudge stood in the doorway of the room. It faced her and presented a row of needle-sharp white teeth. It let out an enormous spitting hiss.

"Huh," Lina said and regarded the small creature. "Aren't you a funny little cat."

The cat hissed again. It was a scraggly thing with skinny legs and visible ribs protruding against a hollowed-out belly. Tufts of fur were missing from its lean body, and the long black fur it did have was matted and uncared for. Lina tilted her head to the side before rummaging around for some dried meats among her things. The cat regarded her quietly with a striking indigo gaze.

"Here." Lina fumbled over. "Have some." Her voice felt strange and unused as she spoke. She shook the meat in midair, and the cat looked at her quietly before baring its teeth again. It gave a fantastic growl before running the other direction in a fluid scamper. Lina sighed and placed the meat in the hallway before bundling herself back up and sitting by the fire.

She ended up sleeping like that in her nest of blankets and pillows on the floor as the fire died down for that night. She was sore in the morning, but when she went into the hallway, she discovered that the meat she left was gone.

She smiled to herself and started whistling on her way out.

∞∞∞

In the fifth month, she shivered and hacked her way through the worst of the winter. She learned to chop firewood herself alongside learning to pick splinters out of her fingers. She named her new feline friend "Cranky" for how she wandered around the empty castle grounds hissing at everything that so much as twitched.

In that sixth month, Lina was talking to Cranky almost

every night. She told her bedtime stories and made-up riddles and laughed at the way that cat curled her kinky tail around her body. The cat's ribs disappeared into a soft, round belly within the passing weeks as Lina fed her, and she stopped trying to turn Lina's fingers to ribbons. Lina, herself, kept waking up with tears in her eyes, but that was neither here nor there.

The outside world soon started to thaw. Birds returned to the trees, and grasses started pushing up through the snow. Lina had made it an entire winter by herself without getting morbidly ill or freezing to death. She threw a small party for herself in the cellars of the castle. She celebrated by making Cranky an oatmeal bath for her sore skin and putting on a pair of thick oven mitts and dumping her in. The cat yowled and fussed and almost scratched the daylights out of her, but her fur started growing back with some more ointment applied to the scratchy red areas. After that, Cranky sometimes sat at the end of Lina's bed and purred when she thought Lina was asleep.

In the seventh month, *he* arrived. It was early spring, and Lina had lost track of the dates. She was in her small garden in the courtyard, trying to tend to a wilting tomato plant when a voice, a new voice, a different voice, called out to her.

"PRINCESS ELLINA."

She froze.

"I'VE COME FOR YOU."

Lina straightened up and turned around rapidly as if to find her own tail. *Am I hearing things?* she thought at once. *Is this the final stage of loneliness or madness?*

She was in a muck of her own worries when someone clanked into the courtyard and spread his arms wide. He wore a polished set of silver armor with the insignia of a gray wolf on the breastplate. That had to be the Menthias family from the south. The slits of his helmet were tilted up to reveal a freckled fair face with a tuft of red hair falling into the eyes. He had acne blooming just above his thin eyebrows and a bright expression.

Lina regarded him in awe.

He must've had taken her silence as a good sign as he

beamed in her direction. He gave a low bow that had obviously been practiced for many years. "I am Prince Gordon of Menthias," he announced to someone who was not listening. "I come bearing liberation for you, my lady!"

"Uh." Lina was still trying to process a separate other person in her midst. "Excuse me?" She was proud of herself for not hissing on sight as Cranky might've done.

"Look, look." He struggled for a brown bag slung around his shoulder and just out of reach. "It took me, like, several months to get, but it should do the trick."

Lina froze. "Trick... for what?"

His face grew somber. "Of course, I'm sorry to bring it up right away. I'm sure it's still a sore subject."

"Right." Lina wasn't completely sure this wasn't a vivid hallucination. Had she taken her tea wrong this morning?

"My family sends our highest regards and most sincere condolences. We will send our best men to take care of that nasty snake once everything is settled." He sounded genuinely enthusiastic, though his voice broke on a word or two as he spoke.

"Uh." Lina looked around awkwardly, afraid she'd been mistaken for some other exiled princess. "Snake?"

"Right, again, sorry." He flinched. "Sore subject."

"Why are you here?" Lina was short on manners. Even after all those months of longing for company, she also found herself wanting to return to tending her tomato plant.

"To cure you!" He threw his arms out wide. "From the snake bite that made your skin poison."

Lina's mouth fell open. He looked practically ecstatic at her reaction.

"I know! You must think there is no cure, but boy do I have something for you." He finally managed to extract a single brown bean from his bag. "Here!"

Lina must've eaten something truly fetid to be having this dream. She took a step back. "Listen," she said slowly, "I'm not sure what you're thinking—"

"You just have to eat it."

"What?" She wrinkled her nose. "Eat it? I mean..." A spark of hope flared in her chest that she quickly squashed again. "How do you know it will work?"

"Well, I was told by a witch that it would. And it was very expensive." He grinned as if that solved everything. "And then we can seal our victory with a kiss, and this horrid affair for you shall be over."

Lina narrowed her eyes at the suggestion. She took a step back. "How old are you?"

He seemed to hesitate for the first time. A crease formed between his eyes. "I'm sure your parents will be pleased it's me instead of, like, Prince Mavin from the Fiore Islands or something," he grumbled. "It'll be a nice wedding. My parents are already getting the florists ready."

Wedding? Wedding! Wedding. Lina decided to turn around at that moment. "Thanks," she said stiffly, "but I should, um, go."

"Princess," the young knight said as he took a step toward her, "a witch guaranteed this bean would cure you of any and all that ails you."

He took another step toward her. Lina retreated toward the nearest staircase.

"That's nice?"

"Don't you, uh, not want to be poisoned anymore?"

She regarded the magic bean skeptically. "Really, that's sweet."

"My family's really keen on having you." His armor clanked as he moved.

"Sure."

"We emptied a good deal of coin for this bean. You just have to try it." He was jogging now, and Lina was streaking in the opposite direction. "Princess!" he called, but she was darting up a set of stone steps and into the bowels of the castle. "It's good, I promise!"

Lina found herself maneuvering up and down stairs in the echoing long stone halls until she found a crack in one of the walls. She pushed her way into the enormous hole and cut through thick cobwebs and things crawling near her feet. She held her breath and hid for an hour while listening to the prince call for her.

"Magic beans?" she murmured to herself. "Really?" She had no idea how to make sense of his other suggestions. A snake? Poison? Marriage? Surely, she had missed a key carrier pigeon about this. The prince was clanking around the castle for days afterward. He had to be only fifteen, and he was not very quick. He never managed to find her or convince her the bean was anything but expensive snake oil. Finally, he left on the morning of the fourth day.

He left the bean with a note. Lina regarded it coolly for several hours before pouring some water on the bean itself. A gash opened up in the middle of it, and it started to sing a noisy opera where it lay. Cranky stuck her head in to investigate before Lina bashed it with a shoe and decided she was right not to trust random boys carting magic beans around.

She thought she was done after that—a fluke, perhaps, or a fever dream that was best left to ignore.

A second man appeared on a sunny morning in what Lina was informed to be April. He opened with poetry dedicated to her red hair, which seemed very misguided seeing as her hair was brown. He was middle-aged and pot-bellied with an impressive mustache that flared out at the tips in a perfect curl. Sir Wycan of the Western Kingdom of Doun. He offered her a pair of red slippers that could dance away any wickedness that befalls you.

Lina had a much shorter conversation with him before she decided that she hated poetry and had no interest in trying on any red slippers that may or may not be colored with blood. This knight also appeared to believe she had been bitten by an enchanted snake.

Sir Wycan was much more persistent than the teen who arrived, and he set up camp in one of the castle courtyards. He only left a week later when the rains tore down his makeshift camp and he cursed her to the high heavens.

"You can't be this choosy!" he bellowed as he went toward the doors. "We had a good offer for you."

After her months alone, Lina wasn't certain she remembered language very well and simply watched him go. The only good thing about Wycan's visit was that he left his camp supplies behind, and she rifled through his things. A poster was among his discarded belongings. She read it slowly.

WANTED

The words said.

KNIGHT TO BREAK THE POISON ON
THE PRINCESS OF CARDWIN
REWARD: HER HAND IN MARRIAGE

Lina balled up the piece of paper and tossed it into the fires. She turned to her adopted cat with a grunt. "This was my parents' plan?" she said and poked the fire viciously. "This was what they've been working on?" It was like finding out her birthday present for that year and every year after that was going to be socks with holes in them.

A third knight arrived as the days were growing thick with humid heat. She barely gave him the time of day when he offered her a lumpy magic lather. None of the knights seemed particularly good at hearing "no," so she hid from this one too. He only lasted a day before departing with his entourage back to where he came.

"The king of High Mountain is coming next!" he called loudly. "And he won't be as nice as I am."

Lina was left alone again, and some part of her assumed that would simply be the rest of her life—hiding and avoiding and being alone. There was a drizzle of dank, misty rain the day the fourth knight arrived. Lina was out in the forest gathering mushrooms when she heard the clip-clop of horse hooves along the road.

"Another?" she muttered. Perhaps she would never know any rest after that due to her parents' whims and terrible planning ability.

Lina didn't bother combing her hair out or making her drab dark dress any more presentable as she slipped toward the path to intercept the new knight. "I'm not interested!" she called loudly. "You're at the wrong castle."

This knight was riding an enormous black horse with a braided mane and a spiked war saddle. The horse looked exceptionally well-bred with a shiny coat and tall stature; Lina might've even liked to meet the animal on a different day. The misty rain coated her skin, and she wiped her hands down on her skirts.

This knight was smaller and had on dented armor with rust at the joints and a visor pulled all the way down. Perhaps he was on some sort of quest on a budget. There was a hummingbird on the chest plate and a great blue plume coming out of the helmet. Lina waved her hands again to get the rider to stop. "This isn't the right place."

The horse trod to a halt, and Lina came up alongside them. The knight cocked his head to the side.

"We're closed," she said stubbornly. "Please turn back now."

The rusted helmet clanked, and Lina pondered sending this poor knight home with a sandwich or something at least. She opened her mouth to announce again that she wasn't interested in whatever this new knight was selling. The knight instead gently kicked the horse's sides and kept riding to the castle.

"Must you all be like this?" she grumbled before going around the back to return to her rooms and hopefully ignoring the visitor. She had been dallying in more books on medicine and had begun hoping maybe there was a cure for her after all. It would help if she had some books on magic, too, but all she had was a single fortune-telling book that she had read cover to cover. She wasn't sure if cloud interpretation was going to save her anytime soon, however.

She checked up on the knight a few times as he seemed

to make camp in the courtyard like all the others. He started small fires and peered up at her and sometimes walked the halls methodically. He never addressed her at any point or offered her a cure, so Lina tolerated the weird knight's presence for several long days.

It was only after a week that she decided she didn't like whatever this new arrangement was. "He can't really keep staying here," she talked to her cat mindlessly. "What is he even eating?" She stopped in a doorway. "Do you think he's terribly ugly? Is that why his visor is always down?" Cranky did not respond. "Maybe he's a ghoul." She shuddered and found her way to the courtyard.

To her surprise, the knight's supplies were bundled up and put back on the horse.

"Good," a metallic voice came from inside the armor. It echoed and had a delicate timbre to it. "You're here."

"Yes, yes, I'm here," Lina said impatiently. "I'm glad to see you are off now. Have a good journey home." She was glad this one turned out to be simpler than the rest.

The knight shook his head. "It's time," the voice announced. "How would you like to be cured, Princess?"

Lina rolled her eyes openly. "More magic beans?" she mumbled to Cranky, who stood at her side, lashing her tail back and forth. Lina addressed the knight again. "I'm afraid to tell you that your journey has been for naught." She had become better at dismissing them. "I am not a science experiment. I don't wish to try your—"

"It's not an experiment," the voice said slowly. It was very rudely sure of itself. "And the cure isn't here. How could it be? It's time to leave."

Lina looked the knight up and down and noticed that the knight had slid back on his saddle as if to allow a second person in front.

"Oh, absolutely not." She turned. "Good day, sir."

"Wait," the voice called as Lina started to hurry to the door. "You need to pack your bags. We need to go, Lina."

"Lina?"

She turned around in a frenzy. At least the others had been respectful.

"That's awfully familiar." She bared her teeth. "I'm not going anywhere with you." She sounded somewhat childish, but she didn't care anymore.

"You can't stay here forever," the knight said softly. "I know how lonely it must be."

Lina's eyes went wide. "You don't know anything." She started stomping away for a final time.

"But how else will you get rid of the flowers?" The words were faint and tickled at the back of her neck like a rash. Lina stopped in place. She glanced over her shoulder. The blood drained from her face.

"How do you know about that?" A haunted feeling crept up her spine. This was not a regular knight.

The knight dipped their head. "I'll show you." It was a whisper. "Come with me."

Lina folded her arms over her chest. "Why should I trust you?"

"Because . . ." The knight tugged their horse toward Lina. "You have no other choice."

Lina snarled. "Liar."

"A king is coming to claim you. The king of High Mountain. He won't take no for an answer."

"Liar!"

"No, Lina," the knight said sullenly. There was something heavy that hung over them both. "Check the roads tomorrow morning. King Darrell wants nothing more but to take your kingdom into his own."

Lina bit her bottom lip. How could she believe a knight like this? How could she give into these nothing words? But somehow, she found herself believing this hummingbird knight.

She shifted from foot to foot. "How do I know you aren't just trying to sweep me away?"

"You don't," the knight said as the horse flicked its ears. "But I promise on my honor I only mean to help you."

I must surely be a fool, Lina thought. She knew better than to give into the sad words of a bad knight in rusted armor. However, she looked down at Cranky and then off toward the roads.

"If I find out you're lying—"

"Pack your bags."

"Fine," she said sharply. "But I am not riding on your horse with you." There was no way she could risk touching the animal anyway. To her own great astonishment, she went back to her rooms and packed a bag.

"Come now, Cranky." She emptied a second bag and held it open for her cat. "I can't do this alone."

It was a testament to the many hours she spent nursing her back to good health that the little black cat walked into the bag. Lina returned to the hummingbird knight, where they gave each other expectant looks. The knight simply gestured, and they began to move. Lina found herself forced to leave her home once again and traverse into the unknown.

"How far is it?" she asked as they exited the enormous castle doors.

"They say it will be four days and three nights," the knight said carefully. "And you must be ready for the challenges ahead."

Some part of Lina's chest fluttered at the word "challenges." She rarely imagined she might be able to go on adventures like the heroines in her storybooks. She had always been cursed and hidden away. There was very little room to dream of a world beyond that.

She glanced at the knight. "Where are we going?"

"Where else?" The knight pointed them toward the east. "East. Into the place it began." They found the dusty main road just as the sun was reaching high in the air. They faced the burned wood with the blackened trees and dead hills. Lina clenched her teeth but forced herself to start moving so at least the knight wouldn't know she was breaking out into a cold sweat. The woods waited with not even a rustle as they entered.

∞∞∞

They passed the first couple hours in a clipped silence of Lina's own making. The journey was surprisingly empty. The land was a rolling darkness with ashen trees barren of leaves and left with terrible burned trunks that reached for the weak sun. It was still gray out, and Lina had a feeling it would remain gray. It was deadly quiet without songbirds or scuffling animals in the mix. The breeze was cold despite the season, and nothing but blackened forest spread before them for as far as the eye could see. It gave her a deep sense of unease that fell into boredom after the long hours passed.

She had a terrible feeling about the knight beside her, as well, but it was too late to creep away now. She was on an adventure. It was well into the fourth hour when her feet began to ache, and her eyes traveled over the big, black horse.

"What's your horse's name?" she found herself asking despite herself.

The knight was going at a grudgingly slow pace to accommodate Lina's refusal to ride with them. "Radish."

"What?" Lina wrinkled her nose. "Like the vegetable? That's . . . that's a terrible name for a horse."

"And what would you name him, Princess?" There was something teasing and familiar in that question that made Lina falter.

"Well, very much not *Radish*," she said with a huff. "What kind of name is that for a war horse? Ooh, everyone fear the radish knight!"

A chuckle came from inside the armor. "I'm afraid you'll have to settle for a radish knight. Though that's not technically my title." The knight tapped the insignia on the chest plate.

"Right." Lina hid a small grin. "Because Hummingbird Knight is *much* scarier."

The knight simply chuckled again, and Lina opened her

mouth to ask for the knight's name but found that she couldn't bring herself to do it. They walked until the shadows grew long and slithering across the ground and the knight announced they had to stop soon and build a fire.

That proved more difficult than it sounded because the hummingbird knight insisted that they couldn't break off any branches from the trees themselves or use any of the knight's own wood yet. They could only use what was already on the ground. That was easier said than done. Lina pricked herself on many wood-shaped objects before gathering enough twigs for a measly fire in their camp. The knight was already sitting by it after finishing brushing and watering Radish the horse.

"Are you going to take that armor off already?" Lina asked pointedly as she sat down with a good distance between them.

"I'm taking the first watch," the knight said, and that was the first time Lina noticed the rapier held in the knight's right hand. The knight was methodically cleaning the thin weapon. Lina hummed quietly to herself before digging out some dried meats and feeding them to Cranky, who had already finished walking in circles and hissing at nearby rocks.

"Suit yourself," Lina said with a sardonic smirk. "Literally, I suppose."

The knight snorted. "Terrible joke, Princess."

She rolled her eyes. "Should I stay up, as well?" she offered. "I can keep you awake with more of my jokes."

"No," the knight said softly. "Go to sleep. You'll need your rest for what is to come."

Lina raised her eyebrow. "What exactly is to come?"

The knight tilted their head toward the smoky, empty woods. "You're not the only thing that's cursed here," the knight said forlornly, and it was about the most ominous choice of words that Lina had found.

"Well, all right then." She reached for her sleeping pack. "On that note, I am going to pretend to sleep and try not to wee myself before our grand adventure."

The knight laughed again, and it sounded throaty and

real. "Noted, Princess."

She set out her sleeping arrangement far from the poor knight and found herself drifting off to sleep almost immediately under the knight's watch.

$$\infty\infty\infty$$

Lina awoke with a deep soreness in her feet and a dull ache spreading throughout the rest of her body. She blinked a couple times before bolting upright as she remembered she was not in her dusty master bedroom anymore. She clutched at her sleeping blanket like she was a child again. The trees were tall, and their wood warped. There was a long moment where she held her breath and felt deeply *watched*. Mist had gathered on the ground, and the morning air was thick and impenetrable.

Lina gulped and stood as she realized she was alone in the camp. "I'm not afraid . . ." she announced to no one. "I'm not afraid of you!" she called loudly before jumping as someone clunked nearby.

"I'm sure the trees aren't afraid of you either." The knight returned and was holding a water skin and a cloth. "Here." The knight offered them both to her.

Lina stared at them bemusedly. "Am I really so dirty after only one day on the road?" She accepted the water skin and washcloth without brushing against the knight's fingers.

"You'll want to wash thoroughly," the knight said mysteriously. "No sweat. No dirt."

"Why?" Lina prompted.

The knight gestured loosely. "Today won't be as easy as yesterday once the road ends."

Lina raised her eyebrows sharply. "The road is going to end?!" She straightened up. "You could have told me that." She was sick of being the least knowledgeable person around.

The knight shrugged and the armor clanked. "You know now. And we'll want to be *quiet* from here on out too."

Lina faced the knight petulantly. "I know your secret, you know," she said because she could.

The knight chuckled from within the armor. "And what's that?"

Lina hitched her skirts up to start washing her legs. "You're a lady knight. I can tell."

The knight laughed again. "Right you are," she said and started packing up the camp. "Though that's not a secret."

"So you can take the helmet off!" Lina felt like kicking things over.

The knight shook her head. "Wash off. Then we go."

Lina flared her nostrils and started undressing the rest of the way. The knight quickly turned to face the other direction as if stung, which gave Lina at least some satisfaction. She shivered in the dull light of the morning and washed off the dust and sweat from the day before. It was still misty and gray by the time Lina collected her cat and they were back on the road.

The day was deathly silent once more and Lina almost felt like crying. This wasn't how she imagined grand adventures going in storybooks. In fact, the cold, dead eyes of the forest watching her was worse than any story she could've imagined.

She turned to the knight again in conversation. "So," she said and kicked a stray stone away, "how does one become a hummingbird knight?"

"By training with a falcon knight first, of course," the knight said easily. "And being more stubborn than not."

"Huh." Lina cocked her head to the side. She didn't recognize the name. "Tell me some of your grand knightly adventures then. Perhaps ones with a happy ending that don't involve cursed forests."

"I will," the knight said. "But first we have to get through our own adventure." The mist had been growing steadily thicker and denser as they walked. The knight halted her horse as they could no longer see their hands in front of their faces.

Lina stood perfectly still and glanced around the damp, chilly air. "Where are we?" she asked with no real weight.

"The road is ending," the knight announced darkly.

Lina bit her bottom lip. She looked down, and the path in front of them seemed to grow thin like spread wool. It was strangely dizzying to look at—and wrong. She squeezed her eyes shut to push the image of it away. There was something off about it.

"Listen, Princess, stay close from now on," the knight said slowly. "You cannot wander off the path after this. I am not exaggerating when I say you will perish if you leave this next road."

She gulped. "There's another path?"

"Of course." The knight reached into her pack. "You just have to know how to look." She took a handful of something and tossed it into the mist.

Lina watched in awe as the mist itself sizzled like a burning thing. Lina inspected the ground and noticed large white crystals. "Salt?" she said with some disbelief. "You're throwing salt at it?"

"Salt," the knight confirmed before tossing another handful of it into the mist and listening to it make a sound like frying bacon. The mist parted little by little and revealed a single path forward. This one was completely white and very slim compared to the path behind them. Lina knelt to inspect it.

It appeared to be made of broken white seashells. "We're nowhere near the ocean," she murmured to herself, and her insides twisted unnaturally.

"Again, walk close to me," the knight repeated before hurrying her horse onto the strange shells ahead. The horse's steps crunched like shattering glass with each movement. Lina looked behind them and pondered escaping and forgetting this entire ordeal.

She faced the lady knight instead and followed her into the mist and onto the white shell pathway. The mist seemed to close in around them and obscure the way back. They didn't talk after that.

Lina stopped in place after several steps as noises returned to the world. A low moaning resembled people on sick-beds or the wind through tunnels. Her skin prickled, and she peered through the mist with squinted eyes.

She barely breathed. Something was bent low in the mist and staggering forward. "What is that?" she hissed as her stomach bottomed out.

She could make out sunken eyes and a bald head. The creature held itself at an unnatural angle and walked with an unsteady gait. Lina remembered herself and started walking again to stay close to the knight. As they drew closer, the thing's skin appeared too tight and tinted a dark blue. It wore shredded rags, and a low moaning sound seemed to come from it.

"What is that?" she hissed more loudly.

"They are of this cursed part of the wood," the knight explained blankly. "Don't worry. They have terrible hearing and eyesight. Only their sense of smell remains, and even then, they cannot find the seashell path," she said with her helmet pointed toward the creature. To the credit of the war horse, it didn't so much as whinny as they passed the unnatural thing. "Some call them the ambling dead."

Lina swallowed, and she gripped her bag more tightly. "A forest ghoul."

She really was in a storybook now.

Lina thought they would never reach the end of the walk on that second day. There were blisters on her heels, and her throat was dry and parched even after every sip of water. It was a distant sort of pain because mostly she was preoccupied with the ambling dead in the mist and the fact that she was alone with a knight. They were very far away from civilization now, and what would her mother say?

She supposed it didn't matter. She was staggering and almost swaying back and forth in place by the time the knight stopped. Lina yawned as they came to a halt. "Where are we even going to camp?" she grumbled as she looked around them.

"Here." The knight hopped down from her horse. "We'll camp on the path itself. But don't worry." There was a hint of humor in her voice. "No one else is coming."

Lina reached to put her pack down and was relieved at the idea of sitting. "This is going to be a very uncomfortable sleep; I can already tell."

The hummingbird knight started unloading logs from the saddle of her horse to build a fire, and Lina shook her head.

"How do you even know that it's nighttime?" As far as Lina could tell, the sky was as gray as it had ever been. It was like entering some sort of twilight world.

The knight shrugged. "I don't," she said simply. "But you looked tired."

Lina huffed. "I could keep going!" she lied.

The knight laughed. "I'll make us some soup for dinner."

They got to work making camp, setting out bedrolls, and listening to each other's breathing and steps crunching on the white shells. There was something tense about the way they moved and avoided one another all at once.

Lina gulped down the soup the knight made and then fed her spare meat scraps to Cranky, who chewed on them furiously.

"So," the knight finally spoke up, "what have you been doing in that dank castle for all these months?"

Now she wants to make conversation, Lina noted irritably.

She cleared her throat. "Learning witchcraft, forsaking my gods, and dancing naked in fields as I see fit," she said flatly.

The knight threw her head back. She gave a thundering laugh that was beyond herself. "You've been having a good time!"

Lina couldn't help but smile. "Yes." She grinned down at her lap as the fire crackled in its makeshift pit. "Plus, learning to make my own tea."

"Your own tea, you say." The knight was clearly teasing her. "That is impressive. Did you do your own dishes, as well?"

Lina turned her nose up. "Well, I didn't just let them pile up for months on end . . . at least, not after the first couple weeks."

"I suppose one must keep oneself busy."

"Yes." She nodded. "That and I mostly read and tried to figure out ways to break the curse."

"Any luck?"

"No," she said and shifted in place. She looked off to the side where Cranky was curled up in a ball. "But," she tried to say more brightly, "I do know how to read palms now. There was a whole chapter on it in my fortune-telling book."

The knight nodded. "You are quite skilled in many things it seems, Princess. I expect nothing less."

Lina got a glint in her eye. "Perhaps I could tell your fortune?"

The knight was quiet for a long moment. "I already know my future, but thank you."

"Oh?"

"I'm afraid so." She seemed to shift away as Lina tried to crawl closer.

"I won't touch you," she promised softly. "All I need to do is to see your hands."

A sigh came from within the helmet. "Why don't I tell you a story instead? You said you wanted to hear my tales," the knight said softly. "I have some good ones."

Lina settled back down. "Fine." She looked away into the dank, thick mist. "But you'll have to let me use my newfound powers at some point."

"Of course," the knight said, and there was something weighted about the words. "Of course, Princess."

Lina sat up straight from the way she said it, and the knight cleared her throat.

"There was once a young knight who went on her first quest for the burning tail feather of a firebird . . ."

Lina grinned and sat back. She always did love a good story, and she found herself melting into the voice of the knight and closing her eyes to the heady murmur of it. Despite the chill and the grayness and the unknown task ahead, Lina felt warm.

∞∞∞

Lina blinked open her crusty eyes the next morning. Her body was made of granite stones, and each foot was one big, fiery blister. The horse was already saddled as the knight was watering him, and the grayness surrounded them from all sides. A shiver went through Lina's insides, and she looked around as if to find any landmarks to ground herself. It was all shapes in the mist and that feeling of being watched.

Lina quickly stood and got ready for the day. *Stay on the path,* she reminded herself of the rules. *Stay close to the knight. You'll be safe.*

They began to walk quickly that morning, and Lina's curiosity itched. "How will we know when we're there?" she asked in a small voice and twinged at still not knowing where they were going.

The knight's armor clinked as she looked down from her slow walk with her horse. "You'll know," she said cryptically. "You'll need to trust me."

"Aren't I trusting you enough already?" Lina grumbled and chewed on her dried breakfast apricot.

"I haven't led you astray yet, have I?" the knight said softly, and Lina rolled her eyes.

"You've led me into a bowl of mush with only the dead for company," Lina complained, but her words soon died in her mouth. There was something on the tepid breeze. A noise of sorts, and this one wasn't a moan. Her eyes darted around. "What was that?"

"Ah," the knight said, "I hoped we wouldn't run into any of these. Stay close."

Lina strayed closer to the horse without touching him, and a cold sweat rolled down her back. The murmuring returned. It sounded like a chanting. A lilting, silky voice that crooned just out of reach. Lina leaned forward, and a light darted among the burned trees. It was a soft blue glow that hovered off the ground and burned like a living star among the charred forest husks.

"A will-o-wisp," she said in a hush.

"Yes," the knight agreed. "You know them. Then you know we mustn't listen."

Lina's mouth became a hard line, and she kept her eyes trained on the path ahead.

"Come, come back to me, Lina," a familiar voice whispered. "I'm not mad . . ." its savory tones went on. "I've only ever wanted to protect you. I've only ever wanted to love you."

"Shut up!" she hissed at it.

"Do not engage with the spirits," the knight grumbled to her.

"It started it," Lina defended and tore her eyes away from the traveling lights dancing just outside the path. They were beautiful in the way that wanted to kill you.

"Lina, you're not broken. You're not wrong," a high-pitched, girlish tone spoke, and Lina froze in place.

"No," she said in horror. She recognized that voice and didn't like it. "Stop," she pleaded helplessly.

The wisp continued, "I'll tell them it's not dangerous. I'll tell them it's fine. You've never been—"

"Oh, I've been drinking the dregs and drinking the shiner. I've been calling on girls who call me a bore." The knight's voice was loud, brash, and uncertain of itself.

"What's that?" Lina snapped her attention back to the knight.

"Come on now, even a princess must know this one." The knight continued to sing, "I'm a long way from home and spending my coins on brothels and bastards and the worst of the lot! The soldier of the kingdom's got—"

"Lina," the spirit light burst out, "we love y—"

Lina realized what she had to do. She entered the song

at almost a full shout. "The soldier of the kingdom's got lout. I've given my sword to every lord, and he's given it back with a shout."

It felt ridiculous to be bursting into song together as the spirits whispered at them, but there were few ways to traverse a cursed forest, it seemed, and this was one of them. Lina found herself smiling bit by bit as she sang along with someone else for a change.

∞∞∞

Lina was too tired to even put her pack out that night. She was shivering badly, and the world seemed to be growing darker with every step into the burned woods. She had never been more grateful in her life to sit down and curl up as the knight made them soup.

"Last night," the hummingbird knight muttered as if that meant something. "Ready yourself."

"Perhaps I should learn the sword in less than a few hours," Lina said sardonically between chattering teeth.

"You won't need it," the knight said lightly. "Trust me."

"I keep trying to." Lina hunched over, and Cranky was hissing at the mist with parted lips as they sat there. The soup, at least, was boiling hot and put some feeling back into her fingertips. The knight told her to drink the whole thing, and she did so happily until the fire worked its magic on her worn-out bones and Lina was semi-alert again.

"How are you holding up, lady knight?" Lina finally asked as they watched the fire flicker.

"Well enough." The knight sat close to her this time but didn't look at her. "Though you should rest."

Lina nodded, but there was something gnawing at her. "We're breaking the curse." She looked into the flames and widened her eyes. "We could break it tomorrow."

"That's the idea, yes," the knight responded. "If all goes

well."

Lina nodded. "I've, well . . . I've never been me without it," she pointed out mostly to herself. "I'm not even sure if I know how to be a non-cursed girl." She looked up and cocked her head to the side. "How did you even learn to break it in the first place?"

"Study," the knight said simply. "And some favors to another knight."

"Why?" Lina pried the word loose from roof of her mouth and let it fall between them. The lady knight did not respond. Lina tossed a seashell at her that uselessly bounced off. "I asked why."

The knight shook her head. She reached for her gloves. "Who cares about the past, Princess?" She unsteadily took off her gauntlets. "Weren't you going to tell my future?"

"You'll let me?" Lina beamed. "Though I will warn you," she said with her eyes trained on the knight's helmet, "the past and the future are much the same."

The knight nodded. "Spoken like a true witch."

Lina leaned over toward the knight's hands, and her heart thudded noisily in her chest. She knew what this meant. She studied the calloused hands of the knight with their many riveted bumps. "You've known a lot of toil and labor in your life," Lina commented dryly.

"Surely, you jest," the knight said mischievously. "Me?"

"I'm not done yet," Lina snapped. "You've known much strife," she continued. "But you've got a soft heart." The knight scoffed and Lina found herself speaking without stopping. "Really. And you've always been too insightful for your own good. Noisy, cheerful, awfully full of herself."

The knight grew quiet.

"You captured the heart of someone at a young age, but something happened." Lina sucked in a deep breath. "And it left a terrible wreckage in its wake."

The knight retracted her hands and bowed her head. "You're not a very good fortune-teller, I'm afraid."

"Oh yeah?" A lump was forming in Lina's throat as she said it. "Then tell me a better future, Mary."

The knight sighed and reached for her helmet slowly. "When did you figure it out?"

"From the moment you mentioned the flowers," Lina whispered. "And then I spent days denying it."

The woman seemed to hesitate when taking off her helmet. Lina reached over and took the hunk of metal in her hands.

"Why?" Lina asked.

The helmet lifted slowly, and the red of the firelight caught the many angles of Mary's lovely face. She had the same round nose and steady brow. Her black hair was chopped short, and her eyelashes were long and elegant. A scar ran along the left side of her jaw in a wicked, jagged line, and Lina smiled at her.

She wiped at her damp cheeks. "I missed you" was all she said because otherwise she'd start bawling like she was twelve again.

Mary gave a hesitant smile. "I was so mad at you," she said slowly. "But not for long."

"I'm sorry." Lina drew back with a jerk. She wilted. "I am so sorry."

"Hey, hey now, it wasn't for long, like I said." Mary reached for her without touching.

"It was never supposed to happen." Lina said forlornly.

"It's okay," Mary said slowly. "God, I was afraid you'd be mad at me, too, actually and start yelling."

"What?" Lina sniffled and tried to smooth her hair down.

Mary rubbed the back of her neck. "Because, you know," she said bashfully. "God, I still feel so bad."

"*You* feel bad?" Lina's voice broke. "I'm the one who got your whole family fired! I'm the one who ruined your life."

"Ruined my life?" Mary made a face. "You think I'd ever get to be a knight if I stayed?" She shook her head. "No, Lina."

A shiver went down Lina's spine from hearing her name in Mary's mouth again.

"I'm the one who messed up," Mary said. "I'm the one who,

you know."

"Was my best friend?" Lina offered softly.

Mary winced and her gaze grew hard. "No. I was one who kissed you and . . . hurt you."

"Hurt me?"

"I researched curses like yours in the Falcon Knight's library," Mary explained. "I realized that there must be a price."

"You figured it out all on your own?"

"I did a lot of research." Mary grinned. "And it doesn't hurt to have a wicked smart mentor."

Lina looked down passively at the ground. "You came for me." Realization dawned on her with a bite. "You really came back for me."

"Of course. I had to race that crappy king all the way here, too, so King Darrel didn't reach you first." Mary was smiling as sharp and sudden as a new day. "I wouldn't just leave you."

"You could've." Lina wished she would stop crying as more tears spilled over onto her gown. "You could've saved yourself and your family and never looked back on mine and our—"

"Hey, hey, hey. If there's one thing I know, it's that this was not your fault. I know that." Mary leaned forward. "I came back for that. I owe you that much."

"You don't." Lina gestured fiercely with her hands. "You can go home. You can turn back. I don't have to ruin your life a second time."

"What?" Mary's expression softened. "And what kind of knight would I be if I didn't save the princess?" Lina looked up timidly, and her traitorous heart clenched in her chest. Mary's gaze lingered on her. "I wouldn't make a very good knight at all if I did that."

Something passed between them, and their eyes met like colliding windstorms. Lina was lost to it. She felt a throng of energy pulse through her entire body, and for the first time in a very long time, Lina wanted something for herself. She wanted the one thing that the fairy queen cursed her to never have.

Maybe just once, she thought, *maybe today it's worth dying for.*

Mary pulled back first. "It's late," she whispered. "You should sleep."

Lina shook her head. "And what?" She sniffed and needed to blow her nose. She attempted a smile instead. "Miss my first slumber party?"

Mary gave a hoarse laugh. "If you insist."

"Tell me another story," Lina said breathlessly. "Tell me your whole life." She wished her eyes alone could convey everything she was thinking and more.

Mary leaned toward her with her gaze amber bright. "I wish I could deny you a thing," she said, and it sounded exactly like the Mary of the past. It almost made Lina cry again. "Once there was a scrubbing wench—"

"Don't call yourself a wench," Lina interrupted immediately.

Mary continued with a laugh. "Once there was a scrubbing wench! And she was a bit of a romantic. She believed in knights and heroes and love and foolishness . . ."

Mary told her a story, and for the first time in a long time, Lina was no longer alone.

∞∞∞

It took a spectacular amount of effort to get up the next morning. Lina unstuck her eyes one at a time and pried her arms from the ground and demanded her legs work. She was sore in every muscle—and some muscles she wasn't even sure were hers to begin with. She heaved and pushed until she was on her feet. Mary was sleeping for once. Her armor was still on (it was difficult to remove, she said), and her face was soft and distant.

Lina tried to savor it for a long and delicious moment.

She turned. She packed her single bag and gave Cranky her last piece of dried meat. "You be good, all right?" she said to her furry companion. "I have to go now. This is something I have to do for myself." She adjusted the pack on her shoulder. She watched as Cranky gnawed on the meat and gave her an empty look. "Goodbye."

Cranky got up to follow, but Lina was quicker. She darted down the path and away from her only friends. If she was going to break the curse, Lina wanted to do it as the only one in danger and the only one who would have to pay the price of magic.

She started walking.

She could hear rumbling behind her. "Lina?" a raspy voice called. Lina started running with her feet crunching against the shells. "Lina, don't!" Lina was sprinting away. She was good at being alone. She needed it.

She could hear Mary's voice and the horse's hooves on the ground behind her. There was no way to outrun a knight on her steed. However, Lina turned quickly away from them, and the mist surged in from all sides like a wall.

"Hello?" she called, but her own voice was swallowed by the grim fog. "Mary?"

She had gotten exactly what she wanted when no one answered her. The sound of horse hooves had disappeared, and the wind was the only thing snapping at her neck. A new moaning arose from behind her. Lina looked down and gasped. She had stepped off the path with exactly half a foot. She turned, swept her hair back from her face, and checked the compass from her pack. She faced east. There had to be something there.

The moaning grew louder, but Lina ducked her head and moved as quickly as she could.

"Lina." The little voices were back and so were the blue lights. "Why do you run from us? We're your friends."

She covered her ears and ran. There was nothing but the pounding ground and the sound of her own thundering heartbeat. She streaked among the twisted, burned trees and rounded one thick trunk after the next. The shell path never appeared again. Lina soon grew tired and thirsty, but she didn't stop.

The moaning grew louder behind her.

"Lina," a voice whimpered just beside her, "we know you. We love you. Don't you want to see your parents again? We can take you to them."

"Shut up!" she growled, and a twig snapped behind her.

Lina turned. That was a mistake. She could peer through the fog just enough to see a dozen or so empty eyes behind her. There were bent, broken bodies with sunken eyes and blue skin and mouths hanging open. The ambling dead were slow but persistent.

"Shit!" She was running then. Perhaps abandoning her only guardian hadn't been a great idea, but she wouldn't want Mary hurt on her behalf ever again. Lina started to streak toward the east, but a hand shot out in front of her much faster than she expected. She ducked under it only to run into another ghoul with its face burned off.

"Ah!" she screamed and dove to the ground. She found a hardy stick there and climbed to her feet. "Stay back!" She swung the stick out with all the force in her weak arms. "Don't come any closer!"

Thunk

The first ghoul went down with a wet thudding sound and collapsed in front of her. The next couple started to amble forward. They were slow, but many of them opened their putrid mouths and moaned in her direction. Lina went pale and started to back up and swing her stick in all directions.

"I'll take you all down!" she roared and hit another with a sickening *whap* across the skull.

Whap, thunk, clamp

She hit one ghoul after the next and beat them back one at a time. They were getting closer, however, and she was breathing hard. She absently remembered the stories. *Don't let them bite you,* they said, *lest you become cursed to walk the world as a corpse as well.*

Lina didn't need to be double cursed.

"Ah!" she yelped again as one gray hand burst forward

with gnarled, blackened fingernails. The world went still and faint. Its fingers brushed against her exposed wrist and her skin burst into yellow daisies. It was beautiful, and wrong, and painful.

The dead stopped. They paused and openly stared at her as the flowers grew.

Lina stopped swinging her stick back and forth. "Wha—"

"Back!" A new voice entered the fray. "Back, you undead beasts!"

Lina turned in circles. "Mary!" she yelled, and just as the flowers fell, so did the ghouls' temporary stupor. They started lunging for her again with yellowed, chipped fingers. However, this time a horse erupted out of the mist.

"Stupid, idiot, fool!" Mary roared at Lina and plunged her sword into the back of one of the nearest ghouls.

"Mary!" she cried out, and Mary reached down to take her hand and swing her onto the back of the horse. Lina was relieved to be found. A ghoul tore at her skirts with its teeth sharpened to points and neck at an awkward angle. Lina kicked it back and was swung up onto the horse. Her forearms sparkled with pain from rubbing up against the beast's skin, but she couldn't find it in herself to care. Something meowed from the saddle bag, and Lina held on tight.

"How did you find me?"

"Those terrible wisps told me."

"How?"

"I gave them something they wanted," Mary said sullenly and then kicked the side of her horse. "Now! We have to get out of here." She swung her sword through the nearest ghoul's face and kicked her horse to a gallop as they plunged through the rest of them. More seemed to stream from all sides. Their dead faces warped and yawned as they tried to dig their teeth in.

"God," Lina lamented, "I've doomed us all."

"Not yet," Mary muttered. "We're almost there." She took out a pouch of something and tossed it into the air in front of them. The mist began to sizzle again and part like the last time.

Mary threw handful after handful of salt in front of them, and the mist withered like a living thing.

"Forest," Mary screeched, and she kicked her horse faster, even as the animal's flank was slick with sweat, "let me bring her! Let us pay penance!"

A wall of burned bramble appeared as if summoned out of thin air in front of them. Lina squeezed her eyes shut and braced herself for impact. She held on just as they rammed forward into the forest's depths. It took a long, hard moment for her to realize they had not crashed into a nest of thorns. It took her another moment to pry her eyes open and gape at the scene around them.

They had escaped.

The mist had disappeared into nothing but wisps on the ground, and the first rays of sunlight she had seen in days dappled across the thin strands of grass. Lina's mouth fell open. There were tree trunks around them and fallen burned wood, but instead of a lifeless, empty space, there were green things. Moss grew over the dead trunks; grass and small plants burst up from the rich, dark soil. A bird called in the distance, and the leaves rustled from small feet.

Beyond the greenery, there was gray mist like a wall, but Lina could feel warmth leaching back into her skin from above. She craned her neck around, and this seemed to be a completely different part of the forest.

"We're here," Mary murmured near her neck. "The heart of the forest."

Lina watched as flowers wilted off her arms from where she brushed against the horse. She gritted her teeth and hopped down to the ground. She landed softly on the grass and looked up toward a gentle hill with a seashell pathway leading up it. The path had reappeared.

"The heart of the forest," she repeated. Her head was swimming slightly, and her limbs were heavier than ever. It wasn't pain that greeted her now, but a thick grogginess that bore down on her. She shouldn't have touched the horse.

Lina swayed in place and looked back to Mary. Mary had sheathed her rapier and taken her helmet off. She swung off the horse elegantly and looked toward the lumpy hill. "There is your challenge, Princess," she whispered with her eyes not meeting Lina's.

"A hill?" She smiled weakly.

"The very heart of the forest," Mary muttered and held onto her horse's reins as he shifted in place uneasily. "All of this was to protect it so it can grow back properly," she explained. "No human can proceed any farther..."

"No human, huh?" Lina blinked several times, and some part of her wished she could just lie down and curl up on the ground. Wasn't this enough? Hadn't she pushed and strained enough? "So," she mused, "you don't think I'm entirely human anymore?" She made Mary meet her eyes.

Mary nodded slowly. "Some plant. Some girl." She stepped back. "I can't follow you past here."

Some plant, some girl. Lina had never thought of it like that. She drew a deep breath. "That's it? I climb the hill?"

"There will be a flower at the top. A purple-and-white striped one," Mary said slowly. "You must pick it and bring it back to us."

"Picking flowers." She looked at her shoes. "I'll be just like my parents, I suppose."

"Lina..." Mary said in a warning tone, and Lina flattened her skirts out.

She started to walk and then paused. Lina turned around and hunched over. She stood stock-still in front of Mary and set her jaw. "If we cure me... will you take the reward?" she asked slowly, and Mary surely had to know what that meant. She had to.

Lina refused to look up as Mary cleared her throat. "Do you want me to?" she asked just barely above a whisper. "Do you want me to accept it, Lina?"

Lina inhaled sharply and turned to the hill. "I'm going to climb the hill now," she announced. "And you better be ready for me when I come back." She flashed a smile over her shoulder. "That's what I want."

Mary gave a small bow. "As you wish," she said in the same voice she had used almost a decade ago. "Anything you wish."

"Okay." Lina's expression softened. She straightened her spine before turning again toward the gentle hill. She started to walk with each step cushioned by the greenery. She closed her eyes and waited for her feet to start burning, her ears to start bleeding, or her world to go out like a light. She took another step and her ears popped.

She looked down, and there was something on her arm —green and soft. She touched it, and it was moss. "Lina!" Mary called. "Hurry!"

Lina looked down and raised her skirts up. Thick, green tendrils were popping up from the tops of her feet. Her shins were covered in vines. She touched her neck, and something rustled there. She was turning into the plant she was always meant to be.

The exhaustion washed over her like a warm bath, but she fought through to walk up the hill. Her hands were covered in thick green moss. Bark formed at her elbows. Her ears started to ring, and she tasted muddy earth in her mouth.

"Forest," she whispered weakly, "I am not my parents." She touched a sapling as she passed it gently. "I am not here to harm you. If anything . . . I will restore you." She wasn't sure what she was saying, but she kept walking.

Something hard formed near her throat, and something drooped off the top of her head. A thin bush sprouted from her shoulder. She gave a sigh of relief. A purple flower was at the very top of the hill. It was beautiful and perfect with stripes coming from a yellow center and a long strong stalk.

Lina bent down and guilt roiled in her guts. "I won't take you . . . without giving something back." She had never tried this before, but Lina closed her eyes and imagined the purple-and-white flower in her mind's eye. She imagined the soft petals and rough leaves and the way the flower proudly raised its head toward the sun.

She bent down and pressed her stiff lips to her pinky finger. Lina opened her eyes again and saw a purple flower had sprouted in the exact place she had kissed. She gave a faint smile. "Who knew?" She plucked the purple flower from the earth and gently pressed her own back in its place.

She had no way of knowing if her replacement was enough, but her thoughts were growing distant from her, and she could no longer wiggle her toes. She turned back to Mary, who was shouting at her, but she couldn't hear it. Lina stood with what little strength she had left and teetered down the hill.

Mary's words reached her with every step. "That's it. You're doing it. Come back. Come back to me."

Lina was lightheaded by the time she collapsed at the ground by Mary's feet. Her mouth was all soil, and her body was covered in a layer of foliage she had never seen before. "I'm sorry," she rasped, and she wasn't even sure if the words came out. "I failed."

She closed her eyes and expected to drift away onto a sea of her own making.

"So," a deep voice said with a type of serenity, "you've brought me my heart."

Lina managed to open her eyes again with a great effort and twisted toward the source of the noise. She had barely noticed that her cat had leaped down onto the ground and was standing before the purple flower that Lina had dropped.

"Yes," Mary growled at the cat. "We've brought you your heart. Now accept it, fairy witch."

The cat padded closer to the flower with a flick of her tail. She seemed to unhinge her jaw and devour the flower in one unsightly movement. She took the flower whole and started to glow from the inside out. A brilliant light flashed like the pulse of a small sun, and something morphed and grotesquely writhed within the light.

A new creature stepped out of it with enormous purple

wings and a face of all sharp angles and a frigid, remote beauty. She had silvery skin like the moon with a long black cape draped over her body, and the same deep indigo eyes of a cat named Cranky.

Lina made a small mewling sound from the ground. "You." She couldn't tear her eyes away. "The fairy queen."

"The daughter of Soledad and Cyrus." The queen's voice was thick and otherworldly. "How you've grown." It was almost a joke with the green plants still sticking out of her skin.

"You." Lina licked her cracked lips. "You've been watching me."

"No. You're the one who came to the outskirts of my home and took up residence." The queen peeled her lips back. "You're the one whose family cursed me and made it so I couldn't even return to my own heart."

Lina's head throbbed, and she could barely comprehend the words themselves. She gave a shallow smile. "You always were so cranky."

"Yes, and I should kill you where you lie for your snub and your family's destruction of my home."

Lina found some fire left in her. "Kill me?" She gave a hollow laugh. She had nothing left to lose. "You meant for me to die ages ago, a slow and painful death from flowers. Flowers!"

The fairy queen's face split into a grin. "I said I *should* kill you, not that I would." Her hands twisted over each other. "You nursed me back to health without question. I owe you a debt now, and for that I won't strike you down. Consider yourself"— she bowed—"forgiven."

Lina clenched her hands and lifted her chin up one last time. "Free me," she said with venom dripping from her words. "Free me from these plants!"

The queen tutted. "I can't reverse it," she announced darkly. "You will fade just like the flowers your parents sent me as *condolences* for spurning me the first time. Consider yourself spared."

"Ah!" Lina roared and barely managed to get back to her

feet with the last of her strength.

"Wait," a voice said clearly and cut above the fray. "What about my debt?"

The fairy queen looked up as if noticing Mary for the first time. "A little girl playing knight. What debt?"

"I gave you the flower." Mary smirked and came forward. "I set up this quest to restore your body to you." She put her hand out. "You owe me a favor."

The queen's mouth twitched, and her fists shook. She snarled openly and flapped her wings in irritation. She looked at Mary with utter disgust. "It appears I do. What do you want, girl? And don't ask to reverse your lover's curse. I can't reverse it."

"Mary!" Lina hobbled toward her. "You can ask for all the gold in the world. You can ask for—"

Mary put her hand up. "I know what I'm asking for." She rolled her shoulders back. "I know my future."

The queen simply raised a single eyebrow. "Speak."

"Let me share it!" Mary cried. "Let me share my life-force, share the burden of the curse. Let it no longer be a curse. Let me free her!"

"You want that burden?" the queen asked reproachfully. "You want to share in her folly?"

"Yes!" Mary put her hand out. "Give it to me. Let us beat back this wretched thing. Let me make it not a curse at all."

"That's almost sweet." The fairy queen put her hand out as well. "Almost." They shook with a firm grip and Mary grunted after a moment. "So be it. Have the girl for yourself." She smirked coldly as Mary hunched over. "Win the day, win the girl, share her life-force." Another flash of light burst forth, and the fairy queen was gone.

Mary curled in on herself and Lina's skin started to tingle. Life returned to her limbs and the moss started to peel back from her hands. The greenery fell from her face and bark detached from her elbows.

Lina started to crawl toward where Mary was huddled on

the ground and put her hands out. "Are you okay? Oh God, Mary. What have you done?"

Mary turned toward her with a grimace. "What any best friend would have."

"Best friend?" Lina gave a sad little laugh. "If that's how you want it."

"I do." Mary drew in a deep, shuddery breath. "And the rest of it. All of it."

"Ugh, you stupid, stupid girl." Lina's eyes were full again, and she swallowed thickly. "How could you?"

"How could I not?" Mary croaked. "I mean, I had to prove I liked you somehow."

Lina gave a weak laugh. "I bet you still won't like me tomorrow."

"Bet I will."

"Bet you'll be sick of me after five days of running the kingdom."

Mary chuckled weakly and reached for her. Lina winced back. "I bet we'll have a long, long life to find out about it."

Hot, wet tears ran down her cheeks. Her whole body shook and heaved with it. "Don't," she moaned. "Don't come any closer."

"It's all right." Mary gently took her hand, and it was perfect and too much. "It's over now."

Lina winced, but her hands remained human and unmarred by snapdragons and hyacinth. She made a burbly little noise. "It can't be," she said softly and looked up. "This can't be happening."

Mary shook her head. "Try again, Princess."

"Princess?" She tossed her head back. "I thought you wanted to see the flower thing."

"I've seen it." Mary was drawing closer and closer. "I have to say, I'm not that impressed."

"Then let me impress you." Lina's mouth was tugging up at both sides, and she was flying, floating. She was everywhere and nowhere at once. "Let me show you something nice."

She closed her eyes. She leaned forward. And she pressed her mouth to her favorite person. A warmth like spring spilled through her; it filled the bottomless well in her chest that she didn't even notice was emptier than a desert well. Color flooded back into her chalky skin, and her body tingled with a pulse of new life.

Mary came in soft and delicate like a sunbeam through a rosy window. That kiss took Lina in its hands and shook her to her core until she was that kiss and nothing more. A rose burst from the back of her head, but it didn't hurt this time. It simply bloomed and fell away unnoticed.

Lina squeezed Mary's hand. "I'll have to get used to that."

Mary kissed her cheek softly. "Don't worry, Flower Queen," she murmured. "We have time."

Lina was surrounded by daisies and roses and a world of growing things as they kissed again. And she was full.

About The Author

Jacquelynn Lyon

Jacquelynn Lyon is an emerging author in fiction and poetry. She was born in Boulder Colorado and spent several years as a semi-feral child in the Rocky Mountains. She writes fantasy, science fiction, gay romance, and about anything that fills her with wonder. When not writing she spends her time jogging, reading, and watching her cat do a delightful number of cat things.

Support the author at patreon.com/insomniacarrest

CPSIA information can be obtained
at www.ICGtesting.com
Printed in the USA
LVHW081717241022
731426LV00004B/891